Just Joshua

JAN MICHAEL

THE O'BRIEN PRESS

DUBLIN

First published in English in 2003 by The O'Brien Press Ltd,
20 Victoria Road, Dublin 6, Ireland.
Tel: +353 1 4923333; Fax: +353 1 4922777
E-mail: books@obrien.ie
Website: www.obrien.ie
First published in Dutch by Uitgeverij Leopold
as *Ik Ben Joshua* in 1996.

ISBN: 0-86278-818-8

British Library Cataloguing-in-Publication Data
Michael, Jan
Just Joshua
1.Group identity - Juvenile fiction
2.Children's stories
I.Title
823.9'14[J]

1 2 3 4 5 6
03 04 05 06 07

Editing, typesetting, layout and design: The O'Brien Press Ltd
Author photograph, page 2: David Winner
Printing: Nørhaven Paperback A/S, Denmark

for

Sebastian Adams

CHAPTER ONE

Joshua lay on his back in the warm sea, his eyes closed. At this moment his father was killing the pig. He'd watched once. The pig had looked at him with misery in its small eyes, eyes that were rimmed with lashes as long as his own. And when it had wriggled and shrieked it had sounded almost human. After that, Joshua made sure he was out of the house whenever a pig was to be butchered.

The sea rippled under him and salt water splashed across his mouth. He spat it out. His stomach gurgled and he opened his eyes. Above him wisps of early morning cloud were being stretched aside like elastic, leaving the sky clear and blue.

'I'll be back as soon as it's killed,' he'd promised, making his escape.

'Mind you do,' his father had answered, taking rope down from a nail to tie up the pig. 'I'll need you afterwards.'

Joshua didn't mind helping out afterwards – when the killing was over.

He really ought to be heading home, but he lay there

a little longer, being rocked by the waves, his shorts ballooning up in the air. He tried not to think of the pig, but the slaughter flashed into his mind just the same. After he tied up the pig, his father would slice off its ears. It was the custom, he said. It was so that the pig could not hear the moment when its life left it.

'Go in, Joshua,' he muttered to himself.

He flipped on to his front and swam in from the deep water, letting the breaking waves carry him with them, till his stomach scraped the sand. Then he got to his feet and walked out of the sea. The water had dragged his shorts halfway down his skinny hips and they were full of sand. He shook his legs to dislodge the grains, hoisted his shorts back up to his waist and tightened the drawstring. The hot sun beat down on his back, drying his skin. He shrugged on his shirt, ran up the beach and on to the dirt road, scuffing up puffs of dust which joined the sand that stuck to his legs.

When he reached the clearing it was deserted. The fishermen had set out hours ago and the inhabitants of the small houses that were scattered between the coconut palms around the edge of the clearing had not yet emerged to begin their day. His father always chose the early morning to kill the pigs. No one was around then. No one had to hide their eyes from what he was doing.

Their house was on the far side of the clearing, with a sturdy table set in front of it. On the table was the pig, not moving, dead. Good, Joshua thought.

Now his part in the ritual began.

As he approached, a chicken scuttled out of his way, clucking loudly, and a thickset man with shiny black hair looked up at the sound. His father. He bowed gravely to his son. Joshua bowed back. Still in silence, his father passed Joshua a white bowl.

Joshua took it to the end of the table and squatted down. He dipped his thumb in the bowl and pressed it into the earth. Then he tipped the bowl till blood trickled into the hollow. Using his thumb, he drew a long straight line and then four shorter lines joining it on either side. It took a while to finish the design because the blood dried so quickly. He stood up, bowed to his father and returned the bowl.

As his father took the bowl, a frown creased his forehead and Joshua wondered if he had done something wrong. But his father wouldn't say anything until the ritual was over. He stepped back a pace and turned the bowl upside-down. The rest of the blood drained into the dusty earth at his feet and spread out in a large, irregular stain.

Joshua went to the other end of the table and gripped one of the pig's legs tightly. The animal felt warm under his hands.

His father raised the cleaver in the air. Thud! A leg was severed from the body.

His father breathed out noisily. They could talk now. 'I've told you before, Joshua, you mustn't stand at the pig's head when you give me back the bowl.'

'Sorry.'

'Next time, remember, all right?'

Joshua nodded.

'Okay, then. Now pass me the leg.' The butcher held out his hands and placed the leg on a table behind him.

A cloud of flies rose into the air and dived down again to gorge. His father waved them away. As soon as he stopped waving they came back, as if they were playing grandmother's footsteps.

'Pests!' he exclaimed, irritated. 'I'll be glad when the shop is finished and we can keep the meat away from the flies. Which reminds me, I'll need you to help me with the building later today.' He pointed the knife at the second leg as he spoke.

Joshua gripped it.

'And ask Robert to come and help too, will you?' his father went on, raising the cleaver again.

Thud! The leg came off cleanly.

'Okay.' Joshua turned to go. Robert was his best friend.

'Hey! Not so fast. Help me finish this first.'

Joshua held the carcass steady as his father slid the knife under the pig's skin, slitting it down the side. He had to move his fingers nimbly so as not to get in the way of the knife. His father's hands were big and broad next to his, but they worked quickly and delicately; no one was as accurate with a knife as his father. He was the only butcher in the village. All the other men made their living from fishing.

'They're no good at killing pigs,' his father had told him once when he'd asked. 'They'd botch the job and end up being cruel. They're so used to fish eyes that it doesn't bother them, but I think they find pig's eyes frightening.'

Sometimes Joshua wondered if that was all. Sometimes he thought his father was a butcher only because he couldn't fish. Joshua had never even seen him in a boat.

'Hold the ribs still,' his father ordered. Joshua shifted his hands further up the carcass.

'Ouch!' His hands slipped. A horse fly had bitten his leg. He shook it vigorously, stepping back from the table.

'Watch out!' his father said crossly.

Too late. Joshua had already knocked into one of the buckets containing the pig's innards. He grabbed for it and saved it just before it could topple right over. He pushed it under the table out of harm's way and re-adjusted the cloth protecting it from the flies.

A van drove into the clearing, hooting noisily. A man jumped out of the cab.

'Here.' His father tossed Joshua a coin.

He streaked across and was the first to be handed a loaf of bread from the back of the van.

It was hard, round and still warm, finely dusted with flour. He hugged it to his chest. A bit of the crust broke loose as he walked back to his father. He caught it, put it in his mouth and crunched. It was as crisp as a biscuit. His fingers found the gap left by the fallen crust. He dug into the bread and tore out a chunk, which he offered his father. His father put down the knife, wiped his hands on his shorts and took the bread. He rested his other arm on Joshua's shoulders as he ate. Joshua pulled out another handful for himself.

'Was it a good swim?' his father asked, relaxed now that most of the cutting was done.

Joshua glanced up at him and nodded, his mouth too full to speak. He noticed that his father had forgotten to put his hat back on. He was hardly ever seen without it, removing the battered hat only to go to sleep at night and during the pig ritual. Joshua picked it off the ground and his father bent down for him to squash it on. His father's face immediately looked flatter.

'Thanks, Josh.' All trace of his earlier annoyance had disappeared, and he looked at his son with affection. They made a good pair. Together they stood there, chewing, watching as children and women tumbled out of their houses for the early morning bread.

'Go on,' his father said to him. 'Make us coffee, then you can be off. I can manage for a while.'

Joshua rinsed his hands under the standpipe, shook them dry and carried on round the back to their house and up the steps to the door. The other houses all had doors opening on to the square, but theirs was at the back. Joshua's father said it was to protect them from the flies that were attracted to the meat. Joshua thought it was a strange reason; the flies still came in through the window.

A dog dodged away as it saw him coming, then waited in the shadows, muzzle raised. The dog was old and smelly and an outcast. No one liked him, not really, and he knew it. The villagers called him Swabber.

Inside there was only one room, but that was the case in most of the village houses. In the middle of the floor, between their two beds, stood a shiny display counter that his father had been given and which Joshua was using as a cupboard. From it he took matches, cups, a spoon and two jars and carried them outside along with the paraffin stove. He set the stove down on a bit of level ground, pumped the little lever on the side, struck a match and watched the flame spring into life.

Swabber came and stood at a respectful distance. He wagged his tail tentatively a couple of times, but Joshua ignored him as he put on the kettle, spooned instant coffee from one of the screw-top jar into the cups and then sugar from the other. When he squatted down to wait for the water to boil, Swabber sighed deeply and sat too. Joshua stayed perfectly still, listening to the rattling of the palm leaves over his head and the jumble of voices behind in the clearing. He watched idly as a steady stream of ants marched towards the grains of sugar that stuck to the spoon.

It was a morning like hundreds of other mornings, except that it was the first morning of the school holidays.

CHAPTER TWO

A scruffy bright-eyed mongrel trotted towards the market, past the tailor who sat on the floor sewing, past the metal workshop and the watch repairer. Looking neither to left nor right, it threaded its way through bicycle wheels and long skirts, searching for someone to play with.

Joshua heard the sounds of the market before it came into view.

'Beans! Sweet, juicy beans!'

'You! Hey! How much are the yams?'

'Jamalacs! Only twenty millis a pound! Jamalacs!'

The shouting was tossed noisily back and forth. The dog picked its way down crowded aisles, sniffing ripe fruit and vegetables, tail wagging, still searching.

'Pummel! Oy!'

The dog stopped and pricked up its ears. It doubled back and raced to the low outer wall of the market, where a boy was perched. It jumped up at his knees, barking with excitement.

Robert leaned down and scratched between Pummel's rough hairy ears. 'Hey, Pummel. Good dog.'

By now Joshua had arrived at the market. The village market was as old as he was. The government had built it the year he was born, the same year his mother had died. He prowled round the edges, knowing that Robert would be here somewhere, probably watching the market sellers. Halfway round he found his friend, having a tug-of-war with Pummel over a stick.

'Hello, Robert.'

At the sound of Joshua's voice, Robert looked up. He let go of the stick and Pummel tumbled backwards, surprised at his sudden victory. He dropped the stick at Robert's feet and barked hopefully, but Robert ignored him.

'Thought you'd come,' Robert said to Joshua, talking fast as usual, getting what he had to say out before anyone could interrupt. 'Let's try Mama Calla. She's in the corner over there. I've been watching her.' All the market sellers were women, wearing wraps of cloth that were as colourful as the fruit they sold.

Robert hopped down from the wall and they set off. Suddenly splashes of water hit their feet. A man was hosing down the aisle. 'You two again!' he greeted them. Joshua recognised Simon, a retired fisherman who lived near them. He leaned back from the blast of bad breath from the man's rotting teeth. 'Who are you going to pick on this time?'

'Mama Calla,' Robert answered and Joshua nodded.

'Mama Calla, indeed.' They all looked to where Robert was pointing. Mama Calla was sitting cross-legged, fruit and vegetables laid out on bright blue and orange material in front of her and piled in heaps behind her. She was taking no part in the conversation shouted from one seller to another, but kept rearranging her fruit, moving bananas from left to right, changing the position of a coconut here, an orange there. It looked as if she wanted to be somewhere else.

'In that case … '

The boys squealed as water from the hose hit their legs, blasting away the dust and sand.

'There. At least you'll be clean for her. She's fussy, is Mama Calla.' Simon pointed the hose at Pummel and drove him away before him.

'Wait here,' Robert told Joshua.

Joshua watched Robert saunter down the aisle, his flapping feet too big even for his long legs. He reached the woman's pitch. Joshua watched their heads come together and he tried to follow the gestures they were making with their hands. Negotiations seemed to be going well. A couple of minutes passed.

Robert turned and waved Joshua over.

'One koria fifty an hour, and a paw paw each,' Mama Calla repeated her offer to Joshua.

He glanced at Robert, who nodded. 'Fine,' Joshua said. It was a good deal. Apart from mangoes from their own tree and the odd coconut, they had to buy the rest of their fruit and vegetables from the market.

Mama Calla gathered up her cloth bundle and patted him on the cheek, something he hated. 'I'll be back in an hour or so,' she said. 'Here. A peach for your voice. Sing well.'

Joshua joined Robert on the sacking between the fruit and tucked his legs under him.

'You first,' Robert said.

Joshua bit into the peach, sucked, chewed, swallowed, and took a deep breath.

'Passion peaches, mellow mangoes, paw paw and bananas.'

He paused and went on, singing out even higher.

'Bent bananas, ranel, koli-kutti,'

He was making it up as he went along.

'Ranel, koli-kuttu, anamulu, ripe bananas.'

'We've only got ranel,' Robert objected.

Joshua didn't care. He liked the sound of the names; some of the fruits were really there, others were from a book he'd found dropped in the road and had taken home and studied.

'Mellow mangoes!' he sang out, really getting into his stride now.

'Caraboa, minnie and gundoo. Tamarinds, sweet tamarinds, tamarinds, come buy!'

And they came. His voice rose higher than the women's calls and it attracted customers.

'This is better than hearing you sing at Mass,' Robert said.

'Don't remind me!' Joshua retorted, thinking of the solos the nuns sometimes got him to sing in chapel at school. 'I –'

'Don't talk,' Robert snapped in the bossy voice that he put on for his many younger brothers and sisters. 'I can talk, but not you. You keep singing.'

'They're good tomatoes, Madam,' he said, in his normal voice, to the woman in front of him. She had a tomato in her hand and was sniffing it. 'You won't find any better. Was it a pound you wanted?'

'How much?' the woman asked suspiciously.

'Twenty-five millis a pound.'

'Do you think I'm made of money?' the woman asked indignantly.

'Then take two pounds. Only forty millis for two pounds.'

'Tasty tight tomatoes, Mama Calla's best!' chanted Joshua at his side.

'Who needs two pounds?' The woman considered the offer, shifting her basket to the other arm. 'I'll give you eighteen millis for one pound.'

Robert shook his head. He'd noticed that she had brand new sandals on her feet, and her cloth looked pretty new too. 'Twenty-three millis,' he said.

'Twenty,' she bargained, picking up the tomato she

had put down, scenting compromise.

'Twenty-two,' Robert said firmly. 'It's my final offer. Won't get better tomatoes anywhere.'

She nodded and held out her basket.

'Passion peaches! Minnie mangoes!' Joshua sang.

Robert held up the scales for all to see, put a pound weight in one copper dish and filled the other with tomatoes till the scale balanced. Then he put them down and tipped the tomatoes gently into her basket, careful not to bruise them.

Several women were clustered around the stall now, picking up mangoes and smelling them, prodding watermelons, examining the beans.

'You sing now,' Joshua said, shifting position.

Robert shook his head.

'Ten millis change,' he said to the man he was serving, taking it from Mama Calla's cloth pouch. 'No,' he said. 'You go on. I prefer doing the talking.'

And Robert was better at the bargaining, Joshua conceded silently; he had all the market mamas' patter at his fingertips. 'All right, big feet.' Joshua took another bite of peach and sang on while Robert did the talking and bargaining. They took it in turns to weigh the big green ranel bananas, to slice through melons and pile sweet yellow mangoes into baskets and bags.

They had done good business by the time Mama Calla returned. She weighed the pouch Robert gave her and took two korias and two fifty milli coins out of it, 1.50 korias for each of them. 'Not bad,' she said, 'not bad at all.'

Joshua ducked before her advancing hand could reach his cheek a second time. He jumped across the fruit into the aisle, grinned and took the money, along with the promised paw paw. He put the money in one pocket and the paw paw in the other. 'Come on, Robert.'

'Come back and help me tomorrow!' Mama Calla screeched after them as they squeezed down the busy aisle. 'Mangoes and bananas,' she cried hoarsely, settling herself, 'Tamarinds, juicy tamarinds.' Her cries joined the hubbub of other calls and were swallowed up behind them.

It was just as they were leaving the market that Joshua saw him.

He gripped Robert's arm. 'Look,' he said.

Robert followed the direction of Joshua's gaze. A man was standing a little distance away at the edge of the market, not quite in the shade. He was on his own. People were taking a wide berth around him. No one stopped.

Berries were piled up in a mound on a makeshift table in front of the man: red, golden and black berries, jumbled up together and gleaming. Trickles of juice ran off the wooden board and into the earth, staining it.

Joshua stared. It was very like the stain made by the pig's blood earlier that morning.

Despite the sun's heat, the man wore a blanket around his shoulders. It was striped red and green with a black crocodile woven down the back. He stood perfectly still behind his berries, impassive, indifferent, eyes on the ground.

Joshua and Robert came a little nearer.

The man did not raise his head.

They drew closer still. Joshua crossed himself quickly against bad luck. Robert copied him. As he did so, he stubbed his foot on a stone and sent it flying. The man looked up and almost instinctively reached his arms out over the berries, as if trying to protect them. Sweat was pouring down his face.

'Mountain man,' Robert whispered to Joshua out of the side of his mouth.

Joshua nodded, not taking his eyes off the man. Men from the mountains were rarely seen in their village. They lived high up where it was cool, at least one day's walk away, where the earth was as hard and cracked as this man's skin. Mountain people had their own customs and spoke a dialect that the village people found hard to understand. They kept to themselves and ignored the government, which was down at the coast. Their mountains loomed over the village, as if they were trying to push it off the narrow coastal strip and into the ocean. Perhaps that was why the fishermen distrusted them. They made no secret of their dislike for the mountain people. Joshua hadn't needed Robert to tell him what the man was.

He took twenty precious millis from his right pocket and held the coins out as carefully as if he had been holding out food to a wild dog, his eyes not leaving the man for a moment.

Surprise flashed across the man's face. It passed so quickly that Joshua wondered if he had seen it at all. The man accepted the coins. From the folds of his clothes, he took out a stone scoop and a bag made of newspaper, which he unfolded as if it were a treasure. Slowly and deliberately he dug the scoop into the mound of berries, three, four times, until the fruit filled the bag. He put the scoop back in his pocket, folded over the top of the bag, and handed it to Joshua in both hands, bowing slightly as he did so.

Startled, Joshua bowed back. He noticed, out of the corner of his eye, that Robert was doing the same.

The boys turned and walked away, not speaking. When they had gone about eight metres they stopped and looked back. The mountain man hadn't moved. There he stood, still as a statue, eyes downcast, passive and alone. If it wasn't for the bag of berries in Joshua's hands, their transaction might never have happened.

Joshua unfolded the top of the bag and sniffed.

Robert took a berry, put it to his lips and hesitated. Joshua took one out too. He popped it straight in his mouth and squashed it with his tongue. Strange, sharp, sweet juice spurted into his mouth. He decided that he liked the taste.

The boys walked on till they were out of sight of the man, then perched on stones by the roadside to eat the berries, first in twos and threes, then in small fistfuls.

But the fruit was too ripe for the heat of the coast. They were only halfway down the paper bag when, soaked by the juice, it gave out in Joshua's hands. What was left of the berries plopped to the ground between his feet and lay there, a mushy mess. Joshua and Robert watched in dismay as small red and black ants advanced at once from all sides, as if this was what they had been waiting for all morning. Then larger soldier ants marched purposefully through their smaller cousins to the front of the feast.

Joshua screwed up the bag and licked his fingers clean. 'Let's go and help Dad build the shop,' he said. 'He asked if you would come.'

Robert brightened. He enjoyed himself at Joshua's. There would be just him and Joshua and Joshua's father. It made a change from being at home with his big family and having to help his mother by looking after the smaller children.

'Well, you two,' Joshua's father greeted them. 'Took your time, didn't you?'

Joshua grinned. His father might sound gruff but he knew he didn't really mean it. 'We were at the market.' He remembered the paw paw in his pocket and took it round to the house, where he left it in the shade.

'Now, where do you want us to start, Dad?'

'I'll go on spreading the mortar, you two put on the stones. Use the ones in that pile over there.' He jutted his chin towards a large heap of stones, then turned back to the wall and slapped on some more mortar.

At first Joshua and Robert were slow at finding suitable stones, but they soon speeded up and got into a rhythm where one would be at the pile picking up a stone while the other was putting one down on the growing wall.

'Butcher.'

They all turned. A woman was standing there, basket on arm. 'How about some meat?'

'Of course.' His father hesitated, then passed the mortar board to Robert. 'Here. You say you want to be a builder when you grow up. See what you can do. The secret is not too little and not too much.'

The boys felt him watching them for a moment before he turned away to serve the woman.

Another customer arrived and stood there, talking. Then the butcher was back. He rolled a cigarette and sat down by the wall.

They paused, looked at him. 'No, no, you carry on,' he said. 'I like watching you work. You're doing fine.' He waved the cigarette at them, then lit it. 'Half the pig's gone to the hotel.' He was speaking more to himself than to them, but they caught the satisfaction in his voice. 'And half of what's left is sold already.'

Eventually they stopped and went to squat beside him.

'Here.' Joshua took the coins from his pocket and gave them to his father. 'We helped Mama Calla,' he explained.

'Again?' His father seemed amused. 'Well done.' He pocketed the 1.30 korias. 'Was this all?'

Joshua shook his head. 'She gave us 1.50 each, and a paw paw. But we saw a mountain man, Dad. He was just outside the market. He was selling berries. A pile of them – this big.' He got to his feet and demonstrated. Then he squatted again. 'So I bought some.'

His father looked startled. Then he pulled a face. 'Sour things, those wild mountain berries. I never ... ' He stopped suddenly. 'You didn't like them, did you?'

CHAPTER THREE

A coconut thudded to the ground, narrowly missing a chicken, which jumped in the air and scuttled away, squawking. Joshua's father, spreading mortar on stones, didn't even look up at the sound.

Joshua appeared on the top step of the house, yawning. He scratched his arm absent-mindedly then wandered down the steps and round to the front of the house.

'Can I help?'

Slap went the mortar. His father picked up a stone from the heap and put it down, aligning it carefully. He had almost finished the top of the fourth and final wall.

He paused, took off his hat to wipe the sweat from his forehead, and put the hat on again. 'Yes,' he said, 'After you've made us breakfast. And after you've done the laundry.'

'Oh, Dad.'

'Don't whine, Josh. One of us has to do it, and you can see I'm busy.'

After breakfast, Joshua wrapped the washing inside one of his father's shirts, put the bundle on his head and walked to the bend in the river where the water was shallow. This was where the villagers did their washing. One of the younger women spotted him coming and nudged her companion, giggling. Robert's mother looked up and saw him. 'Hello, Joshua,' she called out to him. 'Come over here.'

He was relieved to see her. She wouldn't make fun of him. He waded in beside her.

She watched him wet the clothes, spread soap on them and rub them hard, pushing and kneading against a nearby rock as he had seen his father do. Then he stood up straight, preparing to beat them. This was the bit he had been looking forward to. He lifted a shirt above his head.

'Wait.' Robert's mother put out a hand. 'Look, like this. Stand with your legs further apart.' She tucked her dress inside her knickers in order to demonstrate. She squeezed out a shirt, whirled it above her head and thwacked it down on the rock, whirled and thwacked, whirled and thwacked. 'All right?'

He nodded.

'Now you.'

She stood back and watched him critically. 'That's it. Not bad at all. Well done.'

He thwacked away, no longer caring that he was the only boy among the women.

A hand in the small of his back sent him headlong

into the water. He coughed and spluttered, rescued the shirt that was starting to drift away, and turned round to see who had pushed him.

Tom and Millie darted behind a rock, laughing. He waded after them as fast as he could, whirling the shirt above his head. They dodged the shirt but he managed to grab hold of Millie. He dragged her, protesting, right into the river and ducked her under.

She came up spluttering, her hands held palm outwards in surrender.

'Wouldn't catch me doing the washing,' Tom teased.

'That's because *you* wouldn't know how,' Robert's mother retorted, before Joshua could say a word. She reached out and trapped Tom as he scurried past. 'Here.' She put a skirt in his hand and began to teach him.

Joshua and a dripping Millie laughed as they watched Tom's efforts.

'Finish your washing then,' Robert's mother ordered Joshua, and winked. 'Millie, you help him. Tom's helping me.'

She began to sing. The other women took up the tune. Joshua, Millie and Tom joined in, pounding the clothes against the rocks, beating time.

When Joshua got back, his father wasn't there. The fourth wall was finished and there was a small heap of mud at the side, still damp, so he couldn't have been gone long. The shop was almost ready; a stone shell. There were still some cracks between the stones that needed to be smoothed over. Joshua scooped some mud up in the trowel and slapped it over the gaps, smoothing it as his father had done. But he soon got restless and wandered off.

At the side of the road he saw Swabber with a rat in its mouth, a large, plump rat of the local sort, which rarely came above ground. The dog shook it hard, his whole body wriggling with the effort, for the rat was about nine inches long.

Swabber dropped his prey, sniffed, licked his lips, then picked the creature up again by its neck, pawing it. At Joshua's approach, the dog growled deep in his throat and glared, trying to be fierce. But when Joshua just squatted in front of him, making no move to take the rat away, he went back to his shaking and pawing.

Suddenly Swabber tired of his game. He abandoned the rat in the dust at Joshua's feet and lumbered off. Joshua noted the dulling, dead eyes, the small pointed ears, the strong claws for digging holes in earth. He picked up a stick and prodded the body to make absolutely sure that it wouldn't spring to life and bite him. When it didn't, he began to unbutton his shirt, but then thought better of it. There was a banana tree nearby and he tore off part of a leaf. Using the stick, he rolled the corpse on to the leaf, folded the ends together and got up, balancing it carefully.

Millie appeared and fell into step at his side. 'Hello, Josh.'

He didn't answer, not wanting to lose concentration and drop the rat.

'What've you got in there, Josh?' she asked.

'A rat.'

Millie gasped in admiration. He should have known it wouldn't put her off.

'Great,' she said. 'Is it alive?'

He shook his head.

'What are you doing with it?'

Since Joshua hadn't yet decided, he didn't answer.

'Josh? What are you going to do with the rat?'

Joshua was still thinking about it.

'Where are you taking it, Josh? Josh? Why won't you answer me?'

Joshua stopped. He had had an idea. He grinned at her. 'I'm going to cut it up. Do you want to help me?' he asked.

'Yes,' Millie said. She was always game for anything.

'You can wear my other shorts and shirt if you like,' Joshua offered.

'Ooh, yes,' she said eagerly.

He had noticed that her dress was starting to tear at the seams. Millie hated dresses, but her mother made her wear them so that it would be easier to tell her apart

31

from Tom, her identical twin brother. She seemed to be constantly growing out of them. Even though she was a year younger than Joshua, she was as tall as he was.

When they got to Joshua's place his father was still missing. The butcher's table was empty, scrubbed clean. Joshua considered using it, but decided that it might not be wise, so he put his package down on the smaller table.

'Ready?' he asked her.

She nodded. 'Your shorts,' she reminded him.

'They're on my shelf,' he said. 'You get them.'

While she was gone, he slid the banana leaf out from under the rat and studied it, first from one side, then the other.

Millie reappeared, dressed in his clothes.

'Hold the rat steady.'

She didn't hesitate.

'First I'm going to cut off its ears,' he announced.

'Why?'

He opened his mouth to explain the ritual. 'So that …' His voice trailed away as he realised that it didn't count. This was a rat, it was already dead, and he hadn't killed it in the first place. Besides, when villagers killed their chickens there was no ritual; they just wrung their necks. The ritual was only for pigs, only for his father.

'Cut off the tail,' Millie ordered, taking advantage of his hesitation. 'I don't like it.'

'Okay. Stand back,' he told her. He brought down the knife with a blow his father would be proud of and cut through the tail an inch from the body – not quite where he'd intended, but almost. With the tip of the knife he flicked it off the table. They squatted down and looked at the wiry, snake-like thing.

'Yuck,' Millie said. 'What do we do next?'

The same as with pigs, Joshua supposed. He turned the rat on its back.

'Hold that leg,' he said and pointed.

Millie gripped the back leg.

'Hold it out from the body.'

Thud!

Down came the knife. Leg split from body. Millie didn't flinch. 'And now the other one?' she asked.

He nodded.

He raised the knife a second time.

His fist was held in an iron grip and the knife pulled from it.

'What do you think you're doing?' Two hands shook him hard. 'That knife's not a toy. It's dangerous. This table isn't for games; it's for butchering. What if that rat had diseases? I thought I could trust you, Joshua. Have you learned nothing? His father drew breath and went on. 'Go inside and stay there till I call for you.' He shoved Joshua from him. 'And you, Tom, go home.'

'Millie,' Joshua heard Millie protest. 'I'm Millie.' But

she didn't push the point. Joshua's father's face was set hard in anger.

Joshua waited for him to go past the window, then threw Millie her dress. He grinned at her, pretending that he didn't care.

'I'll come back later,' she whispered loudly and scampered off.

Once she was gone he sat down on the floor by his bed. He was in real trouble; it wasn't often that his father was this angry with him. He wondered what he would do and how long his father intended to keep him indoors. He reached under his bed for his fruit book. He slid it out and opened it, turning the pages till he got to the spread on berries, looking to see if he could find the mountain man's berries.

'Bilberries,' he read silently, his lips moving, 'blueberries.' None of the pictures looked right, but still he read, enjoying the words. 'Cloudberries.' He took the book on to his bed where the light was better. 'Strawberries.'

He glanced up at the windowsill. A beetle was squatting there. It was bright green and shone in the sunlight like a glittering jewel. He put his head on the sill and examined it from the side. He bent down and blew at it gently. It stayed there, sparkling. He pushed it with his finger, wanting to see it fly.

It flew all right, but when it did it released a stench

stronger than rotting fish, worse than the smelliest lavatory pit.

'Was that you?' his father said, appearing below the window. 'Was it a stink beetle? Did you touch it?'

'Oh,' said Joshua. 'I didn't know. I wanted to see it fly.' It seemed as if he could do nothing right today. His voice faltered, unsure whether his father was still angry. 'It looked so beautiful.'

'Fool.' His father reached up through the window and ruffled his hair.

That was a good sign. Joshua picked up the book quickly. 'Dad. I can't find those berries the mountain man was selling. What are they?'

'They're called …' His father's voice died away. 'Look, I'm thirsty,' he changed the subject. 'Make us some tea, will you? Then you can help me finish off the walls. Go on then,' as Joshua hesitated. 'Hurry up.'

'And no more rats!' Joshua heard him shout as he went to fill the kettle.

CHAPTER FOUR

The sun shone full on the clearing. It picked out specks of dust on the dark green leaves of a mango tree, which swayed as a weight pressed down on its branches. Leaves rustled with movement. Joshua's father approached, dragging behind him large palm leaves that left tracks in the earth. His shadow was only just ahead of his toes at this midday hour. 'Where are you?' he called.

'Here,' Joshua shouted from his perch high above. 'Picking mangoes.'

His father let go of the palm leaves. 'Pass them to me,' he said, 'then come down. I want you to go to the Gola Hotel. Tell Oliver I can take another pig tomorrow if he's got one for me. Can you do that?'

'All right,' Joshua said confidently.

'I'd go, only I want to get on with the roof.' The palm leaves were for the thatch. 'Anyway, I'm sure you can manage on your own. Comb your hair first.'

Joshua didn't bother with his hair, and his father didn't check. He set off down the road that ran along the sea, past the sugar cane and the rubbish tip. He held his nose against the stench. About a mile further along he came to his convent school, a new concrete building, empty now that it was the holidays, apart from the few orphans who lived there with the nuns. The Gola hotel was nearby, beyond the jetty, overlooking the harbour. It was small – two storeys high – its wood painted pale green and white. He thought it was beautiful.

He stood outside the hotel, suddenly unsure of himself. He'd never been here on his own before. A man in a smart cream suit saw him gaping. 'What do you want, boy?'

Joshua jumped. 'Oliver, the cook,' he said politely. 'My father sent me.'

'Go round the back.' The man jerked his thumb. 'That's where the kitchen is.'

Joshua wandered on round, gazing up at the wide verandah on the first floor. Everyone said there were rooms up there for guests, but he'd never met anyone who had stayed there. He wondered what it would be like to sleep in one of the hotel bedrooms, so high up you could look down on the sea.

'Mind where you're going!' He'd bumped into Oliver who was sitting on the kitchen steps, rolling a cigarette.

'Sorry.'

Oliver licked the paper, put the cigarette in his mouth, lit it and inhaled greedily.

Joshua waited.

'Were you looking for me?' Oliver asked at last.

Joshua nodded. 'Dad says, have you got a pig for him?'

'When for?'

'Tomorrow.'

Oliver leaned forward and straightened Joshua's shirt, which had slipped sideways. It was too big for him. It had belonged to his father. He shook his head. 'That's too soon. I can manage the day after. Okay?'

Joshua shrugged. 'I suppose so.'

'Would you like some pastries?'

Oliver's pastries were famous. 'Ooh, yes.'

Oliver stuck the cigarette back in his mouth and got up. Joshua followed him into the kitchen and watched him take pastries from a large tray and put them in a paper bag. 'Here you go, one for you, one for your father. Don't tell anyone.'

Joshua took the other path home, past the hospital. A hospital porter was coming towards him, his arm around a man, half carrying him towards the hospital building.

Joshua almost dropped the brown paper bag.

'Out of the way, you!' The porter barked at him.

Joshua took no notice. He was staring at the man. He was wearing a straw hat shaped like a cone and there was a blanket tossed over his shoulders. The blanket had a black crocodile woven into it.

The man stared back at him. He was so close that Joshua could have touched him. Mountain man.

'Didn't you hear me?' the porter said crossly. 'Out of the way. Can't you see the man's in pain?'

A line of sweat trickled down the mountain man's forehead. Joshua watched as another drop detached itself from beneath the straw hat and glided its way downwards. There was panic and fear in the red-rimmed eyes.

'Why don't you take off the blanket?' Joshua wanted to suggest, but he didn't know the words in the man's language and they stuck in his throat.

The porter elbowed him aside impatiently and led the man past. He stumbled. He looked, Joshua thought, like a puppet whose strings had been cut.

Joshua reached out a hand to help. He touched grease on the man's skin and recoiled. It was smeared on thickly and smelled rancid, like the pork fat his father gave away when it had been standing too long. In one hand the mountain man clutched a string bag that had lumps of blue-grey stone showing through.

The man and the porter finally reached the hospital steps – ten deep steps, white and polished. Another porter hurried down from the building to help.

The mountain man put one foot on the bottom step and paused, swaying and trembling. He looked back over his shoulder and caught Joshua's eyes and held them with his own. He kept his head trained on Joshua as he was helped slowly up the steps, one by one.

Joshua could not tear his gaze away. He began to lift a hand to wave goodbye but found that he couldn't. He was trapped in the man's pleading eyes. It wasn't until the mountain man was swallowed up by the dark hospital entrance that Joshua felt able to move. Then he ran. He ran round the corner of the hospital, down the dusty path at its side, across the flat stretch of grass where coconut palms grew in stately rows, back to the road and on to the edge of the clearing. He stopped outside Robert's house, panting.

'Hey! Joshua!'

He turned and saw Robert under the jamalac tree, helping two of his younger brothers to build a miniature house with broken-up branches and leaves.

'Watch out,' one of the small boys warned crossly as Joshua sat down beside Robert. 'It isn't very strong yet.'

'What's up?' Robert asked over the small boy's head.

'There's a mountain man,' Joshua began and stopped. He wasn't sure exactly how to explain a feeling with facts. 'They've brought him in to the hospital. I saw him. He … looked at me.'

Robert was puzzled. 'So?'

'His eyes … I thought he was asking for help.'

'Help? But he's a mountain man. You just said so.

You can't help mountain men,' Robert said scornfully.

Joshua nodded, then shook his head. 'Maybe this one can get better.'

'Don't be silly. They never do. Mum says government medicine's wasted on them. The only way they come out of hospital is lying down, in a coffin.'

'Yes, but I thought –,' Joshua shifted on the hot ground. 'I mean, let's go back and see if we can do anything.' Suddenly the words were rushing out. 'Maybe mountain people die because they're lonely here and it's strange. And this one had a crocodile on his blanket, like the man in the market. It might be the same man, you see. Maybe we're the only people who know him.'

Robert considered. Then he nodded. 'Okay.' He turned to his younger brothers. 'See you later.' He got to his feet.

Five-year-old Solomon let out a wail. 'What about our house?'

Robert cuffed him gently. 'You finish it and you can show me when I get back. Build a wall of stones around it so the chickens don't peck it over.'

Solomon beamed. He liked building walls. He was already starting to gather stones as they left.

The whitewashed hospital gleamed in front of them.

They drew closer, looking up at the tall windows. Unlike Joshua's house and most of the house in the village, these windows had glass in them, and you could

41

push down the top halves to let the air in. There were ten windows on each side, but they were too high for Joshua and Robert to see in. They prowled around the building, heads craned upwards, gatching glimpses of the black mountains that brooded threateningly behind the hospital, making it look small and vulnerable. A curtain fluttered in the breeze, but no mountain man came to the window.

'I really thought he was trying to tell me something,' Joshua said. 'But how can he if he doesn't know I'm here?'

'Let's go and tell him then,' Robert suggested.

They stared at each other.

'Do you think they'll let us in?' Joshua asked.

'Come on. We'll find out.'

They went round to the front of the building, Robert leading the way. They started up the steps. Joshua stopped and rubbed one foot against the other till he was sure the dust had fallen off. Then he ran to catch up with Robert and together they went into the entrance hall. It was empty and cool. A staircase ahead of them went up to a gallery. The fan set high in the ceiling ruffled their shirts. Joshua stamped his foot and whirled in the wind below it, arms spread wide.

A nun bustled through a door and paused when she saw them. 'What are you two scamps doing here?' she scolded. 'Are you sick?'

Joshua stopped in mid-whirl and grinned at her. 'No,' he said. 'We've come to see the mountain man.'

'Have you indeed?'

'We want to visit him,' Joshua said stubbornly. 'He wants us to.'

She opened a drawer in the desk near the door and took out a file. 'Are you family?'

They shook their heads. 'He's very ill,' she told them gently. 'Only family can visit him, it's the rules.' She opened the file and began to study it.

'Off you go then,' she said firmly, seeing them still standing there.

'Is he dying?' Joshua asked.

She stared at him. 'Didn't you hear me?' she said. This time she sounded cross.

'Yes. But is he? Dying?' Joshua stood his ground.

'Of course not. Now out, both of you. Scram!'

Joshua looked at Robert and they turned.

'Do you think she was telling the truth?' he asked Robert as they went slowly down the steps.

Robert shrugged. 'Not really. Do you?'

'I do,' Joshua said, but even as he spoke, he wondered.

CHAPTER FIVE

Longboats were coming through the breakers. The boatmen jumped into the surf to steady them while other fishermen waded in from the beach to help pull them in. Joshua and Robert watched with the villagers, Joshua still clutching Oliver's bag of pastries. The fishermen jammed rollers under the boats, wrapped ropes around their shoulders and hauled them high up the beach to where a small crowd waited.

Joshua turned away, and, with a wave to Robert, he headed home.

His father was still thatching the shop roof, laying palm leaves across wooden beams and tying them, making sure they overlapped so that rainwater would run off and not come seeping through.

'Oliver gave me some pastries. Look.' Joshua held up the paper bag, crumpled and soggy from being carried around all afternoon.

His father was concentrating on tying one long leaf to another and didn't look down at Joshua till he'd finished.

'Marvellous. Put them in the food tin and we'll have

them with supper. What about the pig? Can he let us have one?'

'Yes, but not tomorrow. The day after. Usual arrangement, he says.'

His father nodded. 'Fine. That gives us another day to work on the shop. Perhaps that's better. Now, I want you to make me a new fly swat, all right? The old one's falling apart.'

Joshua went into the house and stowed the pastries in the tin, pushing the lid down hard to make sure it was sealed. When he came back outside he picked up one of the palm leaves from the ground. He cut a length of stalk and stripped off some side leaves. Then he sat on the new stone bench they had built outside the shop and began plaiting. He worked on the fly swat until the sounds of thatching stopped and he heard his father whistling as he began to cook their evening meal in the yard behind.

After supper he scoured the pan with sand. He rinsed the pan and the dirty plates under the standing tap at the door before bringing his father hot tea. He watched his father take out a small knife and begin to mark a piece of wood with it. The paraffin lamp behind him threw his shadow on the yard. Joshua waited for his father to start to whittle. Once he began carving he seemed to retreat into a world of his own. Joshua slipped away. He knew this was the moment to go.

When he got to the hospital he hesitated, then began to climb the steps. Another nun might be on duty and might let him through, he reckoned.

The entrance hall was empty. He pushed open the door and almost collided with the nun he had met yesterday. She recognised him.

'You again? What are you doing here?'

'I wanted to see if the mountain man wears his hat in bed,' he made up quickly.

'Did you now? Well, out.'

'Oh, please.'

'No,' she said. 'I've told you already, only family can visit. Who are you anyway?'

'Joshua,' he answered, rubbing one foot against the other.

'Joshua,' she mused. 'Where do you live?'

'Back there.' He jerked his head.

'Now I know where I've seen you. Your father's the butcher, isn't he?'

He nodded.

'I see.' She stared at him. 'That's a bit different,' she said.

He looked up hopefully.

'I can see why you –' she broke off. 'Tell you what,' she said. 'If I say which windows belong to his ward, you could keep guard on the outside, couldn't you?'

He hadn't a clue what she meant, but he nodded.

Any information was better than none.

'His ward is at the back of the hospital. There are six windows and his bed is beside the second window from the far left corner. Now go – '

He was already scampering away, eager to locate the window, running down the steps and round to the back.

He found the window and looked up for any sign of movement from inside the glass.

None came.

He waited. He counted to a hundred. Still nothing. He wasn't even sure what he expected, but somehow he had the feeling that the mountain man would know he was there. He counted to two hundred, and then, very patiently, to five hundred. With a sigh he turned to go.

Something caught his eye. Something that gleamed in the moonlight near the oleander bushes. He bent and picked it up; it felt smooth and hard.

He carried his find round to the side of the hospital and stood in the electric light that shone through a window so that he could examine it more closely. It was a snake, carved out of blueish-grey stone. The carving was small and perfect, except for the snake's head, which was missing a tiny chip above one eye. As he gazed at the carving, he remembered the stone in the mountain man's string bag.

He clasped the snake tightly with both hands. It was a sign, he thought jubilantly. He was right. The mountain man *was* trying to communicate.

He returned to the back of the building. Still no one there; no face at the window. He put his fingers to his lips and blew a piercing whistle, the way his father had taught him.

There was no response. Perhaps the man felt too ill to whistle back, he thought.

He raised his right hand high in the air so that the snake could look upwards. Just in case the mountain man was looking. So that he wouldn't be lonely.

He ran home. At the entrance to the new shop he paused, listening, then went in, feeling for the small stack of paper bags his father had been given by Oliver for special customers. His fingers touched them almost at once. He drew out the top one and took it outside. He slipped in the snake and went round the back. His father was still whittling away.

Joshua didn't want to show him the mountain man's snake. He didn't even want to show it to Robert. It was his secret, thrown out while he was there on his own. He went quietly indoors, lifted up the cloth that was draped between his mattress and the floor and laid the snake in the box under the bed where it would be safe and unseen; his father only swept under the beds after the rains. Then he went back outside. He squatted close to his father, picked up a stick and began drawing fantasy creatures in the dust.

That night he turned over on to his stomach and felt beneath the bed. He edged the snake from its bag carefully so that the crackling would not wake his father. He closed his fingers around it and lifted it up to the moonlight. The snake's head reared up from among the thick coils. Joshua ran his finger from the head down along the body and in among the coils; he went round and round until he reached the tip of the tail. The smoothness of the stone against his skin seemed some-how alive. He set the snake down beside his head on the pillow and tried to outstare it, fighting the sleepy drooping of his eyelids. He was sinking now; his back and his legs felt weightless. When his eyelids flickered open for the last time, the snake's head seemed to have grown till it was as big as his own. He slept.

CHAPTER SIX

Old Mama Siska sat at her open door as she had been sitting every day, still as a statue, watching the shop opposite take shape. It was almost ready. In the last couple of days the butcher and his son had moved tables and a meat safe inside. Now her neighbour's son, Robert, was helping. They brought the counter in from the house behind. The boys came out and fixed wire gauze over the window, then they hung a curtain of green fishnet over the doorway to keep out the flies. Now she could see nothing. With great force she spat her wad of tobacco on to the ground, got up and went inside.

In the shop, Joshua and Robert polished the counter till it gleamed, swept the concrete floor and helped Joshua's father fix meat hooks to the ceiling beams.

Twice Joshua almost told Robert about the carving. Twice he shut his mouth again and said nothing.

The next day the pig arrived from Oliver and was killed. Half was set aside for the hotel. His father wrapped up big pieces in banana leaves and then in newspaper and put them in a round, shallow basket.

Joshua put the basket on his head.

'Don't dawdle today, will you. Come straight back,' his father ordered.

Joshua set off at a steady trot for the hotel. He tipped the meat into the box Oliver held out to him and put the basket back on his head. If he was quick, he could go back via the hospital.

'What's the hurry?' Oliver asked, surprised.

'Our shop's opening. Will you come?'

'Sure.'

Joshua had barely waited for his answer before he was running back down the path, heading for the hospital. He ran round and stood under the window, panting. He counted to two hundred. He looked in the sand, under the bushes.

Nothing.

He ought to be going. He whistled. He counted one more hundred.

Still nothing.

By the time he got back, all was ready. His father had arranged the different cuts of pork on the wide shelf beneath the counter. There were sausages too, thick and shiny in their skins, and glistening liver and heart and kidneys, all laid out under a fine net to stop the flies getting at them. There were pigs' trotters, tied together in pairs, and there was fat, which Joshua's father had melted down and put into tins that Joshua had salvaged from the rubbish heap and scrubbed thoroughly. It all looked so smart and new and exciting that Joshua forgot his disappointment over the mountain man.

'We've done well, Josh,' his father said. 'Thanks for all your help.'

Joshua stood proudly beside his father, waiting to see who would be first to visit the shop. It smelled different in here. Outside, the smell of the meat had mingled with the salty breeze from the sea, the hot dust and the scent of ripe fruit. Here there was cool stone, and the tang of newly laid morter made his nostrils tingle. There was no wind this morning; the fishnet curtain over the doorway hung perfectly still.

A figure appeared outside. Old Mama Siska. She shuffled in, pulling the curtain with her. As she reached the counter, the fishnet slid from her shoulders and swung back into position. She peered at the pair behind the counter and made the sign of the cross. Her eyes flickered over the shop, examining it, looking for changes made since the netting on the window and door had blocked it from her eyes. Joshua shifted his feet uneasily. He had never seen her smile, and she wasn't now.

'No meat for me,' she said in a throaty whisper. 'Can't chew it. Anyway, I don't like the stuff. Can't think why you want to sell it.' She paused for breath.

Joshua and his father waited. His father's smile didn't waver.

'I've brought you something,' she went on. Her hands fumbled at her long, wide skirt, plucking at the folds, searching.

'Help her.' Joshua's father gave him a push in her direction.

Reluctantly, Joshua went round the other side of the counter and stood close to the old lady. Mama Siska was shorter even than he was and the cotton of her head-cloth was so old and threadbare that he could see her white hair through it. He thought she must be at least ninety. As she hunted, she mumbled something to herself.

'Can I help, old Mama?' Joshua asked.

She examined him through screwed up eyes. 'Anna's little boy,' she said. 'Yes, you've got her mouth. Pretty mouth. But your hair isn't hers. Or your eyes.'

Joshua glanced at his father for reassurance. People didn't often mention his mother to him.

'She was a good girl,' Mama Siska went on. 'A good girl. Now, what was it I wanted?'

Joshua felt a nervous giggle coming on, but a frown from his father stopped it just in time. 'You were look-ing for something,' he prompted.

'Ah, yes. 'Here ... ' She lifted a fold of her skirt towards Joshua. 'You look for my pocket. Tell me when you find it.'

Joshua went round her slowly, holding her long skirt

out a little at a time, searching for a thickening in the
seam that would indicate a pocket. On the third fold he
found it.

'Here, old Mama,' he said, putting it in her hands.

'Thank you, my darling,' she said.

His job done, Joshua stepped back. He didn't feel
quite sure of himself with Mama Siska, never had.

With a flourish, her hands pulled something from her
pocket and pushed it on to the counter. There was a
rattle of glass. Joshua's father picked up the offering. A
round, lacy cover, with coloured glass beads hanging
from the edges, dangled from his fingers.

'I taught your Anna to crochet when she was a girl.
About your Joshua's age,' she added, almost smiling at
Joshua. 'You have it now. It will be useful for the flies.'

Joshua's father reached under the counter, moved
aside a corner of the net sheeting and put the pretty
cover over a container of fat.

'Thank you, old Mama,' he said, coming over and
giving her his hand as she turned to go. 'That is very
kind of you.'

'It's for luck,' she wheezed, looking up at him. 'For
her sake, mind. You'll need it, meatseller.'

Joshua saw a shadow cross his father's face. To the
villagers, 'meatseller' was a bad word; if they used it at
all it was as a curse. But Mama Siska had said it so
gently that it had sounded more like a warning.

She turned and looked at Joshua. 'Son of meatseller,' she whispered. She crossed herself again, and went out.

He shivered and joined his father behind the counter once more. He opened his mouth to speak, but his father semed so far away that he decided not to and closed it again without saying a word.

A fly landed on the counter. And another. His father handed him the new fly swat. 'They must have come in with her,' he said. 'Kill them.'

By the end of the morning there were lots more flies to contend with; they sneaked in every time the curtain was pulled aside. But there were still far fewer than there would have been outside at the table. Joshua was kept busy swatting them and flicking them on to the floor, in between wrapping up pieces of meat – a bit of liver here, a chop there, a large lump of stewing meat.

Business had never been so brisk. Some people had come to buy, others just wanted to see and admire the new shop. And once they were there they stayed to gossip, enjoying the novelty. It got so full that Joshua was almost suffocated in the press of people.

Someone brought a jar of toddy. Someone else produced five glasses, which were shared out among the crowd. Robert arrived with his mother.

The party spilled out of the shop and into the clearing. A drum was produced, Leon, Robert's mother's boyfriend, began to play a homemade fiddle. Old Mama Siska shuffled forward from the edge of the crowd and was the first to begin dancing, her wrinkles almost relaxing into a smile. The threadbare ruffles at the bottom of her skirt flounced to the swaying of her scrawny hips. More toddy appeared and was passed around.

Children came running into the clearing, including some of the orphans from Joshua's school. Joshua waved to them. Simon, the old fisherman, produced a bamboo flute and began a haunting, lilting tune that the fiddle and drum followed. Another drummer joined them. The band swelled and soon everyone was dancing.

Mama Calla sashayed over to Joshua. 'Give us a song, Joshua.'

Her large body shook and swayed to the music. 'Let's have it then,' she said encouragingly.

He wasn't sure which song to sing, but as soon as he opened his mouth the voice and words just came. The musicians and dancers picked up the tune. Joshua grinned, stamped his feet, weaved and ducked, clapping his hands to the beat.

He halted in mid-turn. The priest was coming across the square, an aspergill of holy water hanging from his hands on a chain. He had come to bless the new building, as was the custom.

Joshua ran over to his father and grabbed his arm. 'Dad,' he said urgently. 'Father Peter is here. Dad!'

His father hastily wiped his lips. He signalled to the musicians to stop and went forward to greet the priest.

'Thank you for coming, Father.'

'Yes, yes,' Father Peter said, waving the thanks away. 'Is that toddy you've got there? Good. I'll have some of that later if I may. Come along now. Show me this shop of yours.' He headed purposefully for the shop entrance. Joshua ran in front of him, pulled the curtain aside and stood back to let the priest in first. His father followed and the crowd squashed in behind. Joshua could feel their breath hot on his neck and the smell of their sweat was strong from the dancing.

Father Peter took the sprinkler from the bronze aspergill and flicked it in one arc, and then another, making the sign of the cross. Drops of holy water flew through the air. 'Bless this shop,' he cried.

Marius, one of the orphans, sneezed and everyone laughed. It was a good sign. The priest dipped the sprinkler in again and flicked water expertly in the direction of each corner in turn. 'Bless this corner; bless the counter,' *flick, flick*, 'bless the window,' *flick*, 'bless the door and those who come through it,' *flick*. Drops fell on the onlookers who hastily made the sign of the cross. The chant swelled. 'In the name of the Father and of the Son and of the Holy Spirit, Amen.'

Father Peter put the sprinkler back in the aspergill and set them down on the counter. 'Right. That's done,' he said briskly. He looked round. 'Now where's that toddy?' he asked, bustling towards the door. 'And music. Let's have more music!'

The crowd surged back outside, Joshua too. He turned and looked back at the shop. Something was bothering him. He went over to the priest. 'Father Peter,' he said, tugging at the priest's sleeve. 'Father Peter.'

'Yes, Joshua, what is it?' The priest turned from his conversation and bent down to him.

'You forgot to bless the outside.'

The priest smiled and started to answer him, but a woman came up and interrupted him, and whatever he was about to say was lost.

Joshua waited patiently for the woman to finish, but then more people came and engaged the priest in conversation. The music had his feet tapping and he could no longer remember why blessing the outside of the shop had felt important, so he went back to the dancing.

CHAPTER SEVEN

The sun came up over the horizon, bright and powerful, throwing shafts of light across the clearing and
catching Robert's head and shoulders in its glare. He
was standing outside Joshua's window, a pebble in his
hand.

A shaft of sunlight passed through the window and
lit up Joshua's foot where it lay outside the sheet. The
foot jumped suddenly as Robert's stone hit its target,
and Joshua sat up with a start. He rubbed the sleep
from his eyes and peered out of the window. There was
Robert, his arm raised, about to launch another missile.

'Get up!' Robert hissed at him. 'The fishing boats are
coming in!'

Joshua looked across the room. His father was snoring in snorts, the way he did shortly before waking up.
He turned back to the window and waved. 'Coming!'

He scrambled out of bed. He picked his shorts and
shirt off the chair where he had left them the previous
night and shook them. A beetle dropped to the floor and
scuttled away. He shook them again. Satisfied that no
more insects were lurking in the folds, he put them on.

He was almost at the door when he thought of the snake. Perhaps he would show it to Robert after all. For a moment he dithered. Then he went back and scrabbled in the box under his bed for the carving. Tucking it under his arm, he ducked beneath the cotton curtain that covered the doorway and clasped hands outside with Robert.

'I have something to show you,' he whispered, opening the paper bag.

'Can't it wait?' Robert was impatient to get going.

'No,' Joshua said firmly. Now that he'd decided to share his find, he wanted to do it straight away. 'Look.' He held it out.

Robert gazed at the snake. His eyes widened. One hand reached out. 'May I hold it?

'Okay.' Joshua shrugged. He watched anxiously as Robert examined the carving, turning it over in his hands and tracing the coils, just as he had done himself. And he felt relieved when Robert handed it back all in one piece.

'Where'd you get it?' Robert asked.

'Wait,' Joshua said. He tiptoed back into the room. His father was still snoring. He put the snake under the bed and went outside.

'Where did you get it?' Robert asked again.

'At the hospital. Where we were looking the other day. I went back. I reckon the mountain man threw it out to try to tell me something.'

'Really?' Robert looked intrigued; this was much more exciting than the fishing boats. 'So let's go there now. Maybe there's another one.'

At the hospital they searched the ground under the mountain man's window, inch by inch. They used their hands as much as their eyes, turning over stones, uprooting straggly weeds. They ducked underneath sweet-smelling oleander bushes and scrabbled among the drifts of dried blossom and leaves on the ground. There was no sign of a carving.

'Hey!'

They turned. Millie was running towards them.

'Shh!' Robert hissed at her, his finger to his lips.

She skidded to a stop in the sand and looked questioningly at them.

'Mountain man.' Joshua spoke in an undertone, jabbing upwards with his thumb.

'We think he's trying to speak to us. Well ... not speak, but communicate,' Robert explained.

Millie looked puzzled.

'He threw me a carving, you see,' Joshua told her.

Millie didn't see at all, but she nodded as if she did. She must tell Tom and see what he made of it.

Joshua felt that nothing would happen while the three of them were there. 'Let's go,' he said.

'No!' Robert's firmness seemed to surprise even

himself. 'We mustn't give up so easily. He just doesn't know we're here. Maybe we can communicate with him. Let's spread out.'

He gestured to his left .'Millie, you stand over there,' he ordered. 'And you stay here,' he said to Joshua, 'I'll stand between you.'

Millie looked uncertain.'What am I supposed to do?' she asked.

'Look up,' he urged her.

Robert might be right, Joshua thought. If they all looked up, it was three times more likely that the mountain man would try to get in touch. 'Think hard,' he whispered across to Millie. 'Make him hear your thoughts.'

Nothing happened, and after a while they went away.

They came back the next day. And the next.

On the fourth day Joshua had to help his father in the shop. By the time he reached the hospital, Robert was already there. So were Millie and Tom, as well as Robert's sister, Miriam. They grinned at each other briefly, not speaking.

Joshua joined their semi-circle in the shade of the oleander bushes where the ground was still cool. He looked at the open window above their heads. The sun bounced off the whitewashed hospital walls, almost blinding him. He screwed up his eyes and stared intently, trying to throw his thoughts out to the mountain man inside.

The white habit of a nun flashed past the window, distracting him. He glanced away. When he looked back, the ceiling fan had been turned on. Its blades clanked, spun, gathered speed and whirred. Watching it spin made him dizzy. His concentration was gone. He ground his left heel into the sand and rubbed his right toes against his ankle where an old mosquito bite suddenly itched. His stomach rumbled.

Tom and Millie had their heads together and were whispering. Joshua took a step towards them.

'Hey, you three!' Robert hissed. 'You've got to think!'

Tom, Millie and Miriam obediently resumed their staring. Joshua scowled. If it hadn't been for him, they wouldn't even be here now, he thought resentfully. But Robert always had to be in charge of everything.

He looked up at the window, the sun blinking back at him from the walls. In the background he could hear the waves breaking on the beach. He must concentrate. He forced himself to picture the mountain man as he had seen him being led in to the hospital. He remembered how the man had stumbled, saw again the fear and the appeal in his eyes. Holding that image in his mind, he tried to force his will through the open window to the patient lying inside.

Now he was able to shut out his friends, the sea, the sun, the building, until all that was left in the world was Joshua and the mountain man.

Something came flying out of the window and fell right at Joshua's feet, kicking up a little puff of dust as it landed. None of his friends moved, but he could feel their eyes on him. Joshua stooped and picked up the blue-grey stone, placing it carefully in the palm of his left hand.

Slowly he transferred it to his right hand and polished it on his tattered shorts. Then he held it up and the others gathered round to admire. The figure had four legs, horns on its head, and the lines etched on its back and sides suggested a shaggy coat. Joshua didn't know what it was. Like the snake, it too was flawed; one of the legs had snapped off at the knee and only a stump remained of the left horn. Millie reached out to stroke the carving.

'Careful!' Joshua said.

'I *am* being careful,' she answered, delicately running her fingers over its head. He watched her jealously and pulled the carving away as soon as he could. All of a sudden he didn't like her touching it. The carving was clearly meant for *him*. He wished he had never shared his secret.

CHAPTER EIGHT

In the early darkness cockroaches converged on a piece of fish that had fallen to the ground. They clambered on top of each other in their haste to get at it, antennae waving wildly. Footsteps approached. The greedier ones, busily gorging, didn't notice until it was too late and a large foot landed on top of them.

Robert felt a crunchy squelch beneath his toes. 'Ugh.' He rubbed his foot hard on the earth to clean off the mess. Round the corner of the shop he could hear water gurgling. He found Joshua at the standpipe, scouring a pan under the tap. Robert stuck his foot under the running water. 'Hello.'

'Oh, hello, big feet.' Joshua picked up another handful of earth and scrubbed it into the pan until it was clean. Satisfied, he rinsed it out.

'Want to come and watch the tourists from the ship?' Robert asked.

'Sure,' he said.

But Robert wasn't listening. He was staring at Joshua's father who was seated on a bench in a pool of light, whittling away at a piece of wood that he held jammed between his knees.

'What's he making?' Robert asked.

Joshua shrugged. As far as he knew, his father had never finished a carving.

Robert went over to him and gazed at the knife, moving rhythmically backwards and forwards, scraping and shaping the wood.

'Please, what are you making?' he asked politely.

There was no answer. Joshua's father didn't seem to notice that he was there.

Robert touched his shoulder and repeated the question, more loudly this time, 'What are you making?'

The knife stopped moving and Joshua's father looked up.

'Making?' he asked.

It was as if he was waking up, Joshua thought, watching. He never interrupted his father when he was carving. He had always felt that he shouldn't. And by now he had become accustomed to his silence in the evenings.

'I'm practising,' Joshua's father answered at last.

'What for?' Robert was polite but persistent.

This time he got no answer. The butcher's head was bent over the wood. Backwards and forwards went the knife, quietly whittling.

Robert beckoned Joshua out of the light and around the corner. 'Why won't he tell me what he's making?' he asked, sounding a little annoyed. 'He must be making *something*.'

'Why must he? He just carves.'

'But he carves every night, doesn't he?'

Joshua nodded, bored. 'Most nights.'

Robert looked thoughtful. 'Perhaps he carves because he hasn't got any friends,' he said.

'Yes, he has,' Joshua retorted.

'Who, then?'

'Well, Leon, and ... Oliver.' He thought for a moment. 'And ... er ... Samuel.'

'They're just people he has to know for his business. They're not real friends,' Robert said, a bit scornfully. 'I mean, you don't see him playing cards and dominoes with them in the evening –'

'He doesn't like games!'

'– or drinking with them,' Robert carried on, ignoring Joshua's interruption. 'And they don't come to see him, do they?'

'When the shop opened, everyone came,' Joshua pointed out, hurt.

'Of course they did. Nobody wants to miss a party, even at the meatseller's.'

Joshua stiffened.

Robert's hand flew to his mouth. 'Oh Joshua, I'm sorry. I didn't mean ... I just meant ... well, he does sell meat, after all.'

Joshua turned on his heel.

'Hey, Josh, where are you going? Aren't you coming to watch the tourists?'

Joshua shook his head and walked away from his friend.

CHAPTER NINE

Under the low circular roof of the millhouse a grey donkey trudged round and round. It was blinkered and harnessed to a long shaft that was connected to the big, flat millstone. On and on it walked, even though there was no one there to make it, not pausing, not slowing down. As the donkey continued in its circle, the mill turned and ground maize into flour.

Joshua kept pace alongside the donkey. He hadn't gone to see Robert at all yesterday, nor had Robert called round to see him. He didn't care! How dare Robert call his father names!

He jumped up to sit astride the shaft close to the animal's neck. Round and round he went too.

The millhouse was where Joshua liked to come to think. No one would bother him here and the farmer wouldn't be back to unhitch his donkey before lunchtime.

Sandwiched between the low roof and the shaft, Joshua could just see a segment of his surroundings as he was carried round in an unceasing circle: here the trunks of coconut tree, there a clump of low-growing bushes. At the opposite curve there was a slice of blue – the sea. Green, blue, bush, sea, round and round they went, calming him and making him drowsy.

A pair of legs appeared in his line of vision. The knees were familiar. And the skirt – Millie. 'Hey.' He was awake at once.

Millie ran over and jumped on the shaft beside him. 'I thought you'd be here. We're going over to Cascas Bay with Dad. You can come if you like.'

'Now?'

'Now.' Millie jumped down and Joshua followed her. He loved going anywhere by boat, especially as his father didn't have one. The world spun. He stopped and waited for his head to clear, then ran after Millie to the jetty.

'Hurry up if you're coming,' her father called to them from the boat. Tom was already there. They ran down the steps and Tom cast off almost as soon as they were seated. Out they went. Millie's father stood in the stern, dipping and raising the oars in short, sharp movements. After a while Tom took over. Slowly they moved parallel to the coastline, heading for the point.

'Have you seen Robert today?' Joshua asked Tom, as casually as possible.

'No,' Tom answered.

Joshua shrugged, as if neither the question nor the answer mattered. He looked back towards the island.

Seen from this distance it was a mass of green. The only buildings he could identify were the few stone houses near the jetty and the hotel a bit further along. Above them, the green grew darker and colder, leading to the jagged, black mountains. Somewhere up there lived the mountain people.

'Josh! Hey, Josh!'

Millie was slapping him on the arm. 'Do you want to row?'

'Can I?' he asked eagerly.

'I just asked, didn't I?'

Johua stood up in Tom's place and took the oars. He tried to manoeuvre them the way he had seen Tom do it. But they were heavy and awkward and he got confused about how he was supposed to move them. The water seemed to be fighting him.

He lost his balance and toppled over. Millie burst into peals of giggles while her father grabbed for the oars and caught them just before they fell ino the sea.

'Millie, you show him,' her father instructed. Seeing Joshua's embarrassment, he turned away, adding, 'I won't look.'

'Put your hands like this,' Millie advised, placing Joshua's hands into the correct position, high up on one oar. Then she clambered round and stood in front of him, grasping the other oar. 'Copy me,' she commanded.

Joshua watched the way Millie worked the oar and tried to mimic her movements. It began to get easier, and eventually he fell into her rhythm; push in, pull up, out, in, push ...

'Let him try again on his own,' her father suggested.

Millie sat down, handing the second oar to Joshua. He did his best, but he soon got hopelessly muddled and had to be rescued again. He felt he hadn't learned a thing.

Millie's father had seen enough.

'Tom, you take over,' he ordered.

He patted Joshua on the shoulder. 'Never mind, Joshua,' he said, sympathetically. 'With your blood, you can't help it.'

Joshua surrendered the oars to Tom and sat down. He wondered what Millie's father had meant by 'your blood'. What was wrong with his blood? Perhaps it had something to do with his father, and the fact that he wasn't a fisherman. He pictured him as he had been the night before, lost in a world of his own, carving. Carving like the mountain man carved. Could there be some kind of link between his father and the stone carvings? That would explain why the mountain man's carvings had come to him ...

'Here, Josh!' Millie was thrusting a rope at him.

'Stop dreaming and tie up the boat to the buoy,' her father told him.

They had reached the point and the yellow buoy that marked the position of the fishing baskets. Tom and his father pulled on a rope and hauled up the baskets, which were constructed of split bamboo. They made perfect fish traps; the fish swam in through the top, but once they were in they couldn't get out again. Today's catch was a good one. They all helped to empty the flapping fish into the boat and then lowered the baskets back into the water.

On the journey home Joshua's thoughts returned to the mountain man. If the carvings had been meant for him, was there something he was supposed to do with them? Or perhaps they had been meant not as a sign but as a gift. Maybe his father would have an explanation.

When he got back, his father was outside their hut, squatting in front of a large log, knife in hand. Curls of wood lay on the ground, gouged out by the sharp blade.

'Dad.'

His father did not respond.

Joshua moved closer. 'Dad,' he repeated.

Still the knife went on, the movements passionate.

Joshua gazed down at his father's head in its battered hat and thought about how he spent every night carving. Robert was right, he realised suddenly, no one came to visit.

To his surprise, Joshua saw that a shape was emerging from the block of wood. Perhaps his father really would make something, this time. He moved round to get a better look at the carving.

His father frowned at the shadow cast on the wood, looked up and saw him.

'I'm hungry, Dad,' Joshua said. ' I've been out on the boat with Tom and Millie. Can we eat?'

His words seemed to break the spell. His father pushed the log to one side and got to his feet.

Soon there were two pieces of pork sizzling in the pan.

'Pass me the salt,' his father said, intent on his cooking.

Joshua picked up a jar and gave it to him.

'Now the plates. And give me the toddy.'

Joshua did as he was told. His father forked meat on to the plates and handed Joshua his. Joshua sat crosslegged on the ground with the plate on his lap.

His father unscrewed the jar of toddy and poured some into a tin mug. He took a mouthful of the drink.

'Dad,' Joshua had a new question for his father.

'Mmm?'

'Why haven't you got any friends?'

A look of surprise crossed his father's face. 'Who says I haven't?'

'Robert.'

'Ah.' He looked thoughtful. His eyebrows came together in the way they did when he was worried or concentrating on some problem. He set down his plate and patted a place on the bench beside him. 'Come and sit here with me.'

Joshua took his plate and sat close to his father; so close that he could feel the steady beat of his heart through the thin shirt.

'Not everyone needs friends, Joshua. I'm happy enough without.'

Joshua digested that. It didn't answer his question. 'But *why* haven't you got any?' he persisted.

'Because I've got you, silly.' His father put an arm around his shoulders and squeezed him hard. 'You're all I need. Now, finish your dinner before it goes cold.'

Next morning Joshua was sweeping the floor of the shop when Robert came in.

'Hello Robert,' his father greeted him. 'Come to do the table for me?'

Joshua barely looked up. He still felt a bit cross with his friend.

Robert brushed past. 'Hi,' he said.

Joshua moved aside to let him by. Out of the corner of his eye he watched him sprinkle sand on the table, dribble water over it, pick up the hard brush and begin to scrub. Joshua's father whistled away as he worked, not noticing the awkward silence between the two boys.

When Joshua had finished the floor he began to polish the counter with a soft rag. His father went out. For a while all you could hear was the squeak of clean cloth on glass and the rasp of Robert's brush on the table.

'I'm bored with this,' Robert said, throwing down the brush.

'No one asked you to clean it.'

'Your father did.'

'Well, okay,' Joshua conceded. 'But you didn't have to come in the first place.'

'Look, I said sorry.'

'You insulted my father.'

'Didn't you hear me? I said sorry. Your father's okay. I wouldn't come here if he wasn't.'

'Why did you come, anyway?' Joshua knew he sounded rude, but couldn't seem to change the way he was behaving.

'If you must know, I came to tell you about the mountain man.'

'Well, what about him?' Joshua asked, trying not to sound interested.

'He's dead.'

'What?' Joshua stopped polishing.

'He died last night.'

'How do you know?'

'I heard Leon say so.'

'How did he know?'

'Maybe from one of the porters.'

'Why didn't you come and tell me?' Joshua felt cheated.

'Come on, Josh, I'm telling you now, aren't I?'

But Joshua hadn't waited for his answer. He was out of the shop and running across the clearing.

'Josh! Wait!'

He stopped for Robert to catch up, then set off again.

'Where are you going?'

'Where do you think?' Joshua retorted. He ran straight up the steps when they got to the hospital, Robert at his heels, and barged into a porter at the top.

'Hey! Where do you think you're going?'

'The mountain man,' Joshua panted.

'What about him?'

'Is it true he's dead?'

The porter just looked at him, not answering.

A nun appeared from behind the porter.

'Is it true?' Joshua appealed to her.

But it was the porter who answered. 'Yes.'

'But he ... I mean –,' Joshua stammered.

'Now calm down. What's it to you? He was only a mountain man, for goodness sake.'

'John!' The nun was shocked. 'We are all equal in the sight of God, John.'

'Of course, Sister. I didn't mean it.'

'You may return to your duties,' she dismissed him.

He turned on his heel and left, not without first pulling a sour face at at Joshua.

'When did he die?' Joshua asked the nun.

'In the night. It was a peaceful death. Now, I have patients to attend to, and I'm sure you two have something better to do than hang around a hospital.' She bustled them out.

The boys walked back in silence. 'What about the carvings?' Joshua said as they drew near the shop, thinking of the stone creatures under his bed.

'What about them?'

'I mean what should we do about them? I'll go on keeping them, shall I?' After all, Joshua thought, they felt as if they were his.

'Sure,' Robert answered airily. He went back to his scrubbing. He said something that Joshua couldn't hear above the noise of the brush.

'What?' he asked.

'I said we'll collect some more next time a mountain man's brought in.'

'And they'll go on being a secret.'

Robert looked shocked. 'Of *course*,' he said passionately. 'They're important, aren't they? Who knows, maybe they're some sort of magic.'

'Maybe,' Joshua agreed.

They grinned at each other, and began to feel friends

again. That night and over the next few nights, Joshua's father carved more purposefully than before. A creature began to form. Its flanks were firm and strong, its snout was stumpy, its tail short and curly. Joshua loved watching it emerge, loved seeing the warm, intent expression on his father's face as he worked on the carving. It was becoming a pig.

CHAPTER TEN

Old Mama Siska peered out from her doorway into the darkness. A light appeared from the back of the butcher's house. Joshua's father came into view, bearing a lamp which he hung on a hook above the shop door. He disappeared out of sight again, and when he returned with his son they were carrying something between them. Mama Siska's eyes opened wide in astonishment. It was a wooden pig; a pig only a little smaller than the real ones that the butcher killed.

They put it down by the doorway. Joshua's father patted its smooth flanks and looked up, eyes narrowed. His face relaxed into a rare smile. 'Yes,' he said, 'it'll look good up there, above the shop. I need brackets, and there are some long screws wrapped in newspaper in the tool box. Will you fetch them?'

When Joshua got back, his father was propping a ladder against the front of the shop. 'Help me bring out the table,' he said.

Together they dragged it out and lifted the pig up on it. His father screwed the pig's feet into a plank.

'Right,' he said. 'Now, you stand on the table.'

Joshua climbed on the table and helped bear some of the weight of the pig as his father climbed the ladder.

'Hold it still.'

It was difficult. Joshua's arms ached and trembled. The carving seemed to take forever to fix. At last the brackets were secure and the screws tightened and the ladder and table were back in their places.

Joshua's father produced a bottle filled with toddy. 'Bring the glasses,' he said.

'The glasses?' Joshua queried. They were for special occasions. They usually drank from tin mugs.

'Of course. We have something to celebrate.'

His father filled his own glass, and then poured two fingerfuls for Joshua. They stood, glasses in hand, his father's arm loosely around his shoulders.

'To Pig!' the butcher said, toasting the carving.

'To Pig!' Joshua echoed, raising his glass and taking a sip. He screwed up his face as the sharp alcohol bit the inside of his mouth and tongue. He handed the glass back quickly to his father, who laughed.

Father and son looked up at Pig in his place of pride, then went to bed, well pleased with their work.

'I'm going swimming, Dad.' Joshua put his head round the shop door the following afternoon.

'Fine. But I want you back before sunset.' His father didn't look up from the newspaper he was reading with deep concentration.

With a glance at Pig, silhouetted proudly against the sky, Joshua ran off to the sea.

When he got to the beach, Robert's mother was there looking out at Leon's old boat bobbing in the choppy water. Joshua spotted Robert's dark head and shoulders, weaving and ducking as he baled water from the leaky boat.

'He's ignoring me,' Robert's mother complained to Joshua. 'Will you go and tell him I need him home to chop wood?'

He nodded, staring at the patch under her armpits where sweat darkened the faded blue flowers of her cotton dress.

'What are you looking at?' she chided him. Her voice was rough but she held out an arm to him and he went and nestled against her, breathing in sweat and soap and the coconut oil she rubbed in her long plaited hair.

'Are you my aunt?' he asked suddenly.

'No.' She looked at him. 'Why? Did you think I was?'

He shook his head slowly. 'Not really.' He drew a circle in the sand with his big toe. 'Have I got any? Aunts and uncles, I mean.'

This time she took more time to reply. 'I'm not sure. I expect so.'

He looked up at her. He thought she was hiding something.

His gaze unnerved her. 'Your mother's family didn't like her marrying your father. At least, I think that's what happened. They never had anything to do with them after that. But you should ask your father about these things.'

'Oh.' He pressed closer to her, enjoying the feel of her fingers in his hair. 'But you could be my aunt, couldn't you?' he asked dreamily.

Her fingers halted, then went on. 'If you want me to be – well, yes.'

'What was my mother like?'

'Your mother?' She thought for a moment. 'She was fun. She used to make us laugh. She – '

'Do I look like her?' he interrupted.

'Bits of you, yes.'

'Which bits?'

'Oh, I don't know. Your eyes, perhaps. Your mouth. You're skinny like her, too.' But she was getting impatient with his questions. 'Now go on. Go and give Robert my message.'

He tore off his shirt and ran into the water, plunging through the breakers and out to the sea, kicking strongly, heading towards the boat. A gust of wind sent the boat swinging round on its anchor to face him as he approached. Two eyes, one painted on either side of the raised bow to guard it from evil spirits, seemed to stare at him as he drew near. He looked back defiantly but then thought better of it and swam away in a circle towards the stern, to haul himself up where the eyes couldn't watch him.

Robert was baling with an old jam tin, filling it with water and sending it overboard in an arc. 'Hello,' he said.

'Your mother says you have to go home and chop wood.'

Robert pulled a face. 'I know,' he said. 'I heard her. I'll go soon. She doesn't need it till later anyway.' He reached for a second tin stowed under the bows and handed it to Joshua.

Joshua looked back at the beach but Robert's mother had gone. He took the tin. Together they dipped their tins in and out of the water in the bottom of the boat. The sun glinted off the bits that hadn't rusted, and shone through the streams of water that tumbled back into the sea. They fell into a rhythm and Joshua hummed as they dipped and threw.

Once they were satisfied that the boat was dry, Joshua balanced on the bows and dived in among the bright shoals of angel fish that flitted through the water. Robert followed him. They scrambled back over the side and dived again, staying underwater for as long as they could hold their breaths.

'I'm going in,' Joshua announced, perched for his last dive, toes curled over the edge of the boat. 'You coming?'

'I want to stay a bit longer,' Robert said. 'Tell Mum I'll be back soon.'

Josua shrugged. 'See you,' he said, and dived overboard, striking for shore. Back on the beach he shook the water from his hair, pulled on his shirt and set off to the point where the path ran inwards to the centre of the village. When he reached the bend that curved round the graveyard he could hear loud and ragged shouting somewhere up ahead. Chickens scuttled towards him, squawking in alarm.

Joshua wondered what was up. Nearer the clearing, he noticed a roughness in the sound of the voices and he slowed down. There was anger, and something else. He shivered despite the heat of the day.

All the men from the village compound seemed to be gathered in the clearing, their backs to him. They were jammed so tightly together that he could not see what the source of the trouble was.

Joshua retreated to the high, bulging root of a tree. He stepped on to it, clutching the scratchy trunk for support, trying to see over their heads.

The men were facing the shop, his father's shop. They shuffled back a step or two in unison, then tightened up again. There was no shouting now.

A cardinal bird sang brightly just above Joshua's head and he looked up for an instant as the flash of red caught his eye. When he looked back, he saw that his father had come out of the shop.

A voice spoke. Joshua couldn't hear what was being said.

His father said something in response.

The crowd answered with a swelling noise that sounded like growling.

His father didn't move.

A man at the rear of the crowd jerked back his arm and threw something. There was the sound of stone on stone as it hit the wall near Joshua's father. Another missile followed.

His father! They were throwing stones at his father!

Joshua jumped down from the root. He ran to the back of the crowd and tried to push his way through, but they were packed so tight that he could make no headway.

'Take it down! Take it down!' the men chanted hoarsely.

Joshua took a few steps back and jumped to try to see what was going on now. His father was setting the ladder up against the shop front.

Joshua ran back at the crowd, braver all of a sudden. 'Dad!' he shouted. He butted one man he had seen throwing a stone. 'Dad!' he screamed. The man stumbled and Joshua was able to squeeze past. Clawing and kicking, he worked his way through the crowd till he was nearly at the shop.

When they saw who it was, the last row parted in silence for him.

His father was at the top of the ladder and had reached the pig. He didn't seem to have heard Joshua. He was fumbling at the brackets holding the pig in place. It was taking him far longer to unscrew them than it had when the two of them had fitted them together the previous night. A screw slipped from his hand and he tried to catch it. A stir in the crowd showed where it had fallen.

Joshua tried to catch the eye of the man beside him, and then the man next to that, but they stared ahead impassively. He turned to the person behind and nudged him. It was Simon. 'Why ...?' he began, but when Simon looked down at him and Joshua saw the anger in his eyes, he fell silent.

The pig was free now. His father stood at the top of the ladder, cradling it in his arms, unable to move. Joshua knew how heavy it was.

'Let me through!' he shouted, his voice shrill.

Two men blocking the doorway to the shop stood aside for him.

Joshua went inside. He tugged at the wooden butcher's table. It moved only a fraction. He tugged again. He could see his father's legs on the ladder outside. They were shaking slightly. He pulled again. A shadow fell on the floor. He looked up. A man stood in the door-way. It was Leon, Robert's mother's boyfriend.

Together they dragged the solid slab outside and set it next to the ladder. Now other men came forward to help. The tension in the crowd was punctured by words thrown out here and there.

'We can't have a pig up there,' Leon explained, avoiding Joshua's eyes. 'It wouldn't die, you see, and then it would destroy our fishing. We caught very little today because of it.'

Joshua had hold of the fore-trotters. Now he took some of the weight of the carving from his father. It was a sad burden. He and Leon carried it inside.

'Sardines mostly, and not a lot of them,' Leon continued.

'Dad will keep it in here,' Joshua told him, touching the pig's head protectively.

Leon nodded.

Joshua watched his father climb down the ladder, tired and bowed and old as he had never seen him before. He carried the ladder round the corner of the shop and laid it on the ground. Then he turned to face the men, his back against the wall. Slowly they drifted away. He sank to his haunches, gazing blankly at the ground. Joshua squatted beside him.

'It's safe, Dad,' he said. 'I put it inside.'

His father didn't respond. Joshua swallowed; he felt cold inside. He began to chatter, about Robert, about the dinghy, how choppy the water was that day, anything that he thought would distract him.

'Psst!' Robert's head showed round the corner, a blur in the gathering darkness.

Joshua glanced at his father. He was still staring into space, and had made no sign that he had heard. Joshua sighed and got to his feet. He felt enormous relief as he walked round the corner of the shop to be with Robert.

'Leon told me what happened,' Robert said. 'Were you very scared? Is your father okay?'

'Yes.' Joshua nodded. 'At least, I think he is.'

'Where's the pig now?'

'Inside the shop.'

'Good. Leon says you mustn't mind,' he went on. 'He says it'll be all right again now the pig's down.'

Joshua scowled. 'What'll be all right again?'

'Well, you know,' Robert looked embarrassed. 'About your father.'

'What about him?'

Robert hesitated.

'What?' Joshua asked again.

'About him being a mountain man.'

Joshua was shocked. 'It isn't true.'

'Only mountain men carve,' Robert pointed out.

'He's from here, from the village,' retorted Joshua.

'But is he?' Robert's voice rose. 'After all, he's not a fisherman, is he? He's a –'

Joshua glared. 'Don't say it!'

'I wasn't going to!' Robert snapped. 'I was going to say butcher. But he *is* different, he's not like us. He must be a mountain man!' he finished triumphantly.

'He is *not!*' Joshua said stubbornly.

'Of course he is. You've only got to look at his hair. It's straight. So's yours.'

Joshua reached up and felt it. He knew his hair was straight, but the significance of it hadn't occurred to him before.

'Mine's curly,' Robert said. 'And everyone else's is too.'

Robert sounded so superior. Joshua didn't like it. He flew at him, butting him in the stomach.

Robert gasped as the air was knocked out of him. He fell to the ground, bringing Joshua down with him.

Joshua tried to punch, but Robert was quicker and grabbed hold of his hands. Joshua struggled to free them, but couldn't. One moment Joshua was on top. The next he suddenly found himself on the ground beneath Robert.

'Mountain man! Mountain man!' Robert taunted him.

'He is not!'

They rolled over and over in the dust. Joshua kicked

and made contact with a shin bone.

'Ouch!' Robert shouted.

Joshua was glad it had hurt. He had wanted it to hurt. 'Take it back! He's not a mountain man. Take it back!' Joshua was on top now. He and Robert had never fought before. At least, not like this. This felt serious.

He wished Robert would hurry up and say he hadn't meant it. He wanted this fight to end. But first Robert had to apologise. 'Take it back,' he urged again, raising his fist.

'All right! All right! I take it back.'

Joshua waited for a moment to make sure that Robert wouldn't go back on his word, but all Robert did was stare up at him. 'Say you're sorry,' he demanded, and instantly regretted it. If Robert refused, he would have to fight him again.

There was a long silence.

'Sorry.' The muscles of Robert's face didn't even twitch.

Relieved, Joshua got off.

Robert scrambled to his feet and brushed the dirt from his shorts.

Joshua held out a hand.

Robert ignored it. Seconds passed. Then, reluctantly, he reached out, clasped Joshua's hand and shook it. 'See you around,' he said curtly and turned to go.

'Rob ... ' Joshua began, but then changed his mind

and decided to say nothing. Maybe it was best to let Robert go.

He sloped inside, lit a candle and held it up to the small mirror that hung from a nail in the corner. He gazed at himself. His pointed chin was different from his father's broad face and his eyes weren't deep set like his father's. But his hair – dark, strong and very straight – was his father's hair. It flopped over his eyebrows, except when he'd been in the sea and could slick it back from his forehead with his fingers. He was shorter than Robert too, but that had never bothered him before. He reached up and felt his hair. Robert was right. He was different.

CHAPTER ELEVEN

Out at sea a cruise ship lay at anchor, white and gleaming, a gangway lowered down the side. Figures descended the gangway to the boat waiting below. When they were all in, it drew away from the ship and crept across the bay, heading for the jetty where Joshua and Millie, Robert and Solomon sat patiently, legs dangling, watching it approach. It was the last day of the holidays.

The boat nudged the bottom step. Tom was waiting. He took the rope his father threw him and tied it fast to a ring. Then he held it still while his father helped tourists up the wet steps and on to the jetty.

There were eleven of them, large men and women, cluttered with hats and cameras, bags and sunglasses. They climbed carefully up the steps, looking around and calling out to each other. They moved slowly down the short jetty in a group. Tourists were always a welcome sight. They didn't come often and they never stayed long.

Tom came scrambling up the steps. 'Come on.' He beckoned his friends to follow. One man in long, tight shorts looked back, saw them tagging along and pointed a camera at them.

Millie began to giggle.

'Don't,' Robert said sternly.

She put one hand over her mouth, then the other, but the giggles wouldn't stop. Tom was the first to catch them from her, then Solomon and Joshua together, and, finally, Robert.

Millie began to imitate one of the women. She pranced on pretend high heels and peered through imaginary sunglasses. The boys rolled in the road, laughing and squirming for joy.

Millie and Tom's father overtook them. 'They're going to the shop,' he told them, jerking his head.

Millie was the first to pull herself together. They followed the tourists into the smart part of the village, beyond the market, near the Gola and the hospital. Millie still succumbed to the odd snort of laughter.

They reached the part where the road was swept every day. You could still see the patterns left by the brooms that morning. A little further on they came to the stone shop that sold local crafts. The tourists crowded inside. The children sat down under a tree to wait, all except Millie who went and stood on a newly painted bench under the window to look in.

'Josh! Come here!' She beckoned furiously.

Joshua and Robert jumped up beside her on the

bench. Since the night of their fight and making up, they'd become somehow closer, and they'd never talked again about mountain men.

Inside, the tourists moved from a display of lace to a pyramid of hand-woven baskets to a selection of pottery ...

'You see?' Millie hopped excitedly. 'Our animals.'

There was a glass shelf full of familiar bluey-grey stone creatures.

'Wow!' Robert breathed. They had never seen so many together. And none of these were broken.

The shopkeeper looked up and glared at them. He waved his arms crossly, motioning them to get down. Millie stuck out her tongue at him.

Joshua tugged at her dress. 'Come on. Down,' he said.

They went and stood at a little distance from the open door, staring in. They couldn't see the stone carvings any more, but they could see that the tourists were bringing things to the counter to be wrapped carefully in shiny paper and tied ceremoniously with string. Singly and in twos and threes the tourists emerged into the sunlight.

The children were ready. Each darted to a different target. Joshua headed for a woman wearing a short dress the colour of cut watermelon.

'Carry your parcel, Miss?' he asked, making carrying

movements with his hands so that the woman would know what he wanted.

She looked down at him. 'Oh my, aren't you sweet? Walter ...' she plucked at the sleeve of the man beside her, 'Walter, isn't he sweet?' Two pairs of sunglasses gazed down at him. Two mouths smiled, showing large, even teeth.

Joshua couldn't understand the words. He smiled hopefully back at them and touched the parcels in the woman's hand. 'Carry them?'

'No, that's okay,' she said, shaking her head. 'They're not heavy.'

Joshua stood his ground.

'Give them to him, Marguerite,' the man said. 'I think it's expected.'

To Joshua's delight, the parcels were handed over.

The group reformed and moved off towards the old leper hospital, with the children in tow. Joshua looked across at Millie who grinned triumphantly at him. They had all managed to get something to carry, even little Solomon clasped a box carefully and proudly to his chest.

From the old leper hospital they trailed to the harbour building and then to the Gola Hotel at the water's edge, where the tourists stopped at the bar for a drink. Joshua gazed up at the winding iron stairs that led to the top floor and its shuttered bedrooms.

'Here.' A hand reached down and took the parcels from him.

Startled, he released them. Just in time he remembered to hold out a hand and smile.

The man raised a camera and it clicked in his face.

'Oh, Walter,' the woman said, 'he is lovely, isn't he. Just look at those eyes. What do you think he's called?'

'Ask him,' the man grunted, turning to go.

She bent down to him, pointed at herself and said, 'Marguerite,' very loudly. 'I'm Marguerite,' she repeated, stabbing her chest with her finger.

She pointed the finger at Joshua.

'Joshua,' he told her, understanding.

'Yoswa,' she repeated. It sounded more or less right, so he nodded, his hand still held out, palm upwards.

'Oh, of course. I'm so sorry.'

He heard her speak, saw her fumble with the clasp of her handbag. She pulled out a purse and took some coins from it and dropped them in his hand.

He closed his hand over them, grinned at her and ran off to join the others who were waiting impatiently.

'How much?' Millie demanded, jiggling about. 'I got two, so did Tom, Robert got one and Solomon three.'

Joshua unfolded his fist. 'Five,' he breathed.

'Wow!'

'Let's get some chocolate,' he suggested. He was feeling generous and wanted to share his good fortune.

He didn't think his father would mind.

Solomon beamed and began to nod. Joshua tapped Solomon's head gently to stop it nodding, took his hand, and off they went, back towards the jetty and to the small shop at the crossroads.

They clustered around the counter where a small display of sweets and chocolates sheltered in the corner furthest from the sun. The shopkeeper sat in the shadows, sipping his tea and keeping a careful eye on his young customers. Joshua's hand hovered over the bars of chocolate, then pounced, picking up two of the same kind. He held out his money to the shopkeeper who relieved him of two coins.

Turning away from the counter, the little group went into a huddle. Joshua pulled off the wrapper from the first bar and peeled back the silver paper. He broke off squares, one at a time, and handed them round. He waited till everyone had finished chewing and sucking and then shared out the other bar, keeping back two squares which he wrapped up neatly in the silver paper and put in his pocket.

'See you later,' he said and ran home. His father was still sitting on a stool behind the counter in the empty shop, exactly as he had left him earlier. There were no customers. Joshua went behind the counter and slid the chocolate along to his father.

'Chocolate, Dad. Look.'

When his father didn't respond, he undid the silver paper and pressed it into his hand. He licked his fingers where the chocolate had melted.

His father swung his head round and looked at him, the dullness in his eyes lifting for a moment.

'You're a good boy.'

'Eat it,' Joshua urged. 'Before it melts. Go on.'

Obediently, his father put the chocolate in his mouth. Joshua waited for him to ask how he had got hold of it.

But his father didn't ask. He didn't seem to be interested. With a sigh, Joshua put the remaining three coins down on the counter and pushed them in front of him.

'Good lad,' his father said. 'Fetch me some toddy.'

Joshua didn't move.

His father's voice tightened. 'Hurry up. It's in the corner.'

Joshua knew very well where the toddy was kept. Since the riot over Pig, his father had been drinking it a lot. There was a mug on the floor beside the jar. He filled it and took it to him.

'No customers?'

What was left of the last pig looked forlorn in the counter. They had thrown some away the night before. Hardly anyone came to buy meat now. Not since the trouble.

'None,' his father answered. 'We'll have to get rid of the lot tonight.'

Joshua went out of the shop, leaving him brooding. He breathed in deeply and began to hum, determined not to be miserable. The humming turned to singing, which gave him an idea. He went into the house, pulled out the box from under his bed and took rattles from it: one was a big matchbox containing hard, red seeds; the other made from half a coconut shell filled with small cowrie shells he'd collected on the beach, with a thin bit of wood nailed down over it. He shook the box and then the shell. The shell was louder and sharper, but both were good rattles, the best he'd ever made. At the doorway he hesitated, then went back inside, picked up the comb from the shelf and pocketed it, along with a thin piece of paper which he folded carefully.

'I'm going to Robert's.' He put his head through the fishnet curtain and told his father quickly, running off before he could be stopped.

Robert and his family were eating. Robert's mother looked up and saw Joshua standing there. 'Hello, Joshua. Come and sit down. Move up, Robert.'

Robert shuffled along the bench, making a place for him. On his other side was Sister Martha, a teacher from the convent where they went to school. She and Robert's mother were cousins. They even looked a bit alike, at least, from what you could see of Sister Martha, which wasn't much – only her face and hands.

Everything else was covered up by her nun's white habit. She offered him a bit of banana from her plate and he took it eagerly.

Robert's mother noticed. 'Haven't you eaten?'

He shook his head.

She sighed. 'Miriam, fetch another plate.'

When Robert's sister returned, she went round the table, taking half a spoonful of rice from one plate, a bit of fish from another, fried plantain from another, till Joshua had a plateful.

'There now,' she said, presenting it to him. 'Eat.'

He put his rattles down on the ground and took it. 'Thank you,' he mumbled.

'He's drinking too much,' he heard Robert's mother mutter to Sister Martha.

Joshua stiffened. He began to shovel in the food.

'It's a shame. At least he'd always been such a good father.'

'He still is!' he wanted to shout. He was pretty certain his father would have given him supper if he'd stayed. At least, he thought so. He put down his plate and wiped his mouth with the back of his hand. 'Hey, Robert!' he called. 'Why don't we go and play to the tourists.' He didn't like to hear his father criticised. He wanted to get away. Now.

Solomon leapt to his feet. 'Yes!' he cried and scampered indoors, Miriam and Tony close on his heels.

Robert groaned when the three of them ran out with an assortment of home-made instruments, jars and bottles and a length of tin lids threaded on a stick. 'Do you lot really have to come?'

'Yes, yes!' they cried, jumping up and down.

'Take them, Robert,' his mother said. 'Sister Martha and Leon and I could do with some peace.'

'Oh, okay,' Robert agreed, grudgingly.

'Yeah!' Solomon cheered.

Joshua was pleased. The more the better, he thought.

On the way, they picked up Tom and Millie. Tom had a tin and a stick, Millie a stick with tins nailed to it that clattered as they walked.

Some of the tourists were gathered outside the Gola, drinks in hand, smoking and chatting. Others sat on tall bar stools on the other side of the open windows.

Robert took charge. 'Sing your market song, Joshua,' he commanded, 'they won't know.' He took Joshua's coconut rattle and began to shake it to mark time. He nudged Miriam who lifted a bottle to her lips and blew across it with a soft moaning sound. Joshua opened his mouth and sang just as he did in the market:

Ranel, koli-kuttu, anamulu, ripe bananas,
caraboa, minnie mangoes and gundoo.
Tasty tight tomatoes,
tamarinds and paw paw.

Passion peaches, mellow mangoes,
bent bananas, buy these too!'

Millie took up Robert's rhythm with her stick of tin lids. Tom pushed his stick through his tin. Solomon blew his bottle then put it down and broke into a capering sort of dance. The tourists didn't know that this was just a market chant, but they clearly liked the sound, so the children played it over again, beaming at each other, pleased at the strangers' reactions. Joshua looked up at the windows of the hotel bar; the woman who had talked to him was leaning over one of the sills. She smiled and waved at him when he caught her eye. The man came into view beside her. She nudged him and pointed and they gazed intently down at Joshua.

'Let's do the river song,' Millie said, 'Can we, Josh? Josh? Will you sing it?'

Joshua looked away from the window and nodded. It was a village favourite. He sang one verse, then put the comb, which he had covered with thin paper, to his mouth and blew. At that point the others joined in, one by one. They played an accompaniment as he sang the next verse. It was a slow, wailing sort of melody about a woman looking for her drowned lover. Joshua concentrated hard on the words. They were so sad, he felt his eyes begin to prick.

Halfway through, the tune changed and became lively. He stopped singing and swapped his comb for

Solomon's bottle and they both played, notes tumbling from them till even the tourists began to jig.

Millie went around with her skirt held out in front and the tourists put coins in it. They finished up with a fishing chant. By this time Solomon was falling asleep and the tourists were fading away, heading for boats to take them back to the ship. Millie shared out the coins and they all went home.

Joshua's father was sitting on their step, one arm thrown around Pig's neck. He stopped stroking it when he saw Joshua. 'Been waiting for you,' he said, his voice slurred from too much toddy.

Joshua put the small pile of coins down on the step.

'G' boy,' his father said. 'You're a g' boy to me.' He began to cry. He stopped and wiped his eyes. ''s time for bed.'

'I know,' Joshua said. He put a hand out to help his father. 'Come on.'

'No,' he said. 'Sit. Move along, Pig.' He pushed the carving along, making room, and patted the step. 'First sit. 've been making decisions. Want to tell you. Sit.'

Joshua sat.

'No more pig,' his father said, 'but plenty of fish, plenty. Most days,' he added. 'I'll smoke whaz over. Smoke it and sell it. I'll talk to whaz-his-name tomorrow – you know, to ... '

'To Leon?' Joshua asked, guessing.

His father nodded. 'Leon. Thaz right. Thaz the man. Going to talk to him 'bout it tomorrow.'

He did too. In the morning, through one half-opened eye Joshua watched his father get up and dress. He even walked part of the way to school with Joshua. When they reached the beach he peeled off, calling to Leon.

Out in the bay, the cruise ship hooted and began to sail away majestically.

When Joshua came home in the afternoon, he gave the shop a wide berth, not wanting to find his father slumped over the counter again.

'Hey! I'm in here!'

He halted and retraced his steps. The counter was empty.

'I've had a busy day,' his father told him, reaching up and vigorously cleaning a meat hook.

Joshua stared. The shop gleamed as it hadn't for weeks. There was only the faintest trace of a meat smell in the air.

'Leon's agreed to sell me the surplus fish. I'll smoke it. I've got a big metal drum to do the smoking in. And I've been to see Oliver at the Gola. He says he'll buy dried fish. Fetch me some fresh water, will you?'

You'll be a kind of fisherman. And you aren't drunk, Joshua thought happily, taking the bucket his father held out to him.

CHAPTER TWELVE

A page torn from an exercise book lifted in the wind and was blown back and forth till it finally settled in a patch of cracked, curling whitewash on a flat stone roof. The ink on the page was smudged and faded. Sounds of chairs scraping on hard floor, of chalk tapping on the blackboard drifted up from the row of classrooms beneath, each one open to the verandah that ran alongside. In the third classroom along, Joshua brushed his hair out of his eyes and fidgeted. He put the point of his pencil into the wood of his desk, his mind only half on the lesson.

'New tribes came up from the south in about 1800 ... '

He dug the pencil in and drew it along the grain of the old wood. He pressed it harder and pulled the pencil down towards him, then up again until it formed a leg.

At his side, Robert nudged him and pointed at the blackboard where a nun was chalking lines and arrows on a map. Joshua copied them quickly into his exercise book, then returned his attention to the wood. He drew a line to the left, bumping over the grooves of an earlier carving of someone's name.

Robert leaned across and continued the picture.

Joshua took over again, beginning to draw a robe. He sniggered quietly.

'Joshua? Well?' The nun was looking straight at Joshua, her eyebrows raised.

Joshua looked up uncertainly at his teacher. He put the pencil down very carefully. 'Er, you asked ... I mean ...' He was floundering.

'How many ... migrations ... were,' hissed the boy on the other side of the aisle.

Joshua looked helplessly at him. He'd only heard a few of the whispered words. He tried to answer the nun anyway. 'Er, two, Sister.'

The boy shook his head and mouthed something.

'Three,' he said, changing his answer.

Sister Mary looked at him steadily. 'If you'd been listening instead of defacing school property, you would have known the answer. Can anyone tell him?' she appealed to the rest of the class.

'Five, Sister,' called out a few voices.

'That's right. Five, Joshua,' she repeated to him. 'There's an empty desk up here at the front. Perhaps you would care to fill it? On your own, without Robert, so that you can attend to the lesson?'

Joshua sighed heavily and got up, gathering his books together.

'And no more decorating desks, young man.'

Joshua drew up the chair at the desk she had indicated and nodded, chastened. He hadn't thought she'd seen.

'Now,' Sister Mary announced, coming down from the teacher's platform, 'I'm going to give out the papers for today's test.' They always had a test on their first Friday back at school after the holidays

A sheet of questions fluttered on to his desk. He put out a hand to stop it and began to read.

'You have half an hour to answer the questions. Do your best.'

Joshua knew the answers to the first two questions – they were easy. Quickly he wrote 'green' and 'head, thorax and abdomen'. But he wasn't sure about the next one: what is the definition of an isthmus? He chewed a bit off the end of his pencil and spat it out quickly, remembering. But in his hurry to get down the answer, he pressed too hard on the paper and broke what was left of the point.

He pushed back his chair and stood up. 'Please may I sharpen my pencil?'

Sister Mary nodded.

Joshua crossed to the other side of the classroom. The folding doors that ran along the length of the classroom were opened back so that there was plenty of air. By the front pillar was an oil drum where they put their pencil sharpenings and other rubbish. He took one of the two razor blades from the shelf above, pressed it carefully into the wood of his pencil and began sharpening the tip with steady, outward strokes.

'Psst!' Robert appeared on the other side of the bin. He reached up for the other blade. They grinned at each other.

'Do you know the answer to number eight?' Robert whispered.

'Number eight? Haven't got there yet. What is it?'

A voice came from the teacher's platform: 'Joshua! Robert! No talking, please. I don't want to have to tell you again.'

Joshua wrinkled his nose at Robert and they went back to their sharpening. But they weren't concentrating. Robert jabbed his blade hard at the pencil. It came away at an angle and sliced into Joshua's elbow.

It happened so fast that Joshua didn't notice the blade going in. He felt no pain. Not until he saw Robert staring at him and saw the blood drip into the waste paper and shavings below.

'Sister Mary!'

The nun looked up at Robert's cry, realised what had happened, and pushed back her chair.

'Oh, Joshua! How could you be so careless, that's what comes of talking at the bin. You know you shouldn't ... ' She was bustling down from the dais, talking all the while. 'We'll have to take you to have it cleaned and stitched. Maybe they'll give you an injection; you might get lockjaw or blood poisoning or something. Come along, we have to bring you to the hospital.'

At the word hospital, Joshua dropped the pencil and blade in the bin and was out of the classroom before anyone could stop him, running for dear life, down the steps and across the yard. Sister Mary in her long habit had no chance of catching him. He was terrified. He didn't want to die. He ran out on to the path and headed for home.

'Whoa!' his father said as he rushed by him. 'What's up with you? Why aren't you at school?' Then he caught sight of the blood crusting Joshua's elbow. 'Oh, Josh, what have you done?' He turned away from the old oil drum where he'd been smoking fish and took Joshua's arm to examine it.

'Ow.' Joshua began to cry. Now that he was standing still, the wound had begun to throb.

'That's a nasty cut. How did you get it?'

'Robert cut me. By accident. We were sharpening our pencils.'

'Couldn't they bandage it up for you at school?'

Joshua shook his head. He didn't want to tell his father about the threat of hospital.

'Well, we'd better clean it up, hadn't we?' He put a

sacking cover over the drum and went to wash his hands at the standpipe. 'Come on.' When Joshua hesitated, he added, 'We need to go to the sea.'

'Not to Mama Siska?' Old Mama Siska often took care of the villagers. 'Or to –' he avoided the word.

'I don't think so. Good, clean salt water will be enough. Almost.' He went inside and brought out the small box of salve that he made himself and they went to the beach, Joshua still sniffing.

Joshua flinched as the salt stung the wound. 'Hold still, it won't take much longer.' His father dipped his hand in the water again and the shoal of tiny fish that darted in the shallows divided and then regrouped as if the giant interruption hadn't happened. 'Now, bend your arm so I can see into the cut.'

Joshua did so.

'It's very deep.' His father smeared salve around the wound, then took a handkerchief from his pocket, worn but clean, and tied it tightly around the elbow. 'There. That'll do.' He cupped water in his hands and pressed it to Joshua's face. 'Better now?' he asked, stepping back.

Joshua managed a smile.

'Come on, then.' His father put an arm round him and led him home. 'Here.' He gave Joshua half a mango and brought Pig outside. 'Sit quietly with Pig for a while and eat this.'

Joshua rested his arm on Pig's back as he slowly chewed the juicy mango.

His father went over to the oil drum to see how the fish were coming along. He lifted the poles that lay across the top. Fish hung down from the poles by string threaded through their gills. The first two rows looked ready. Satisfied, he slid the fish on to a metal tray. 'Put these inside, would you,' he asked Joshua.

Joshua got up and took the tray inside, laid the fish out under the counter and brought back the tray.

'Now, would you – ' His father broke off, laughing. 'I forgot, you should be back in school. Go on now.'

Sister Mary was waiting for him on the verandah outside the classroom, looking worried. 'There you are at last. We have to get that cut seen to properly,' she said, eyeing the bloodstained handkerchief around his elbow. 'You didn't think I'd forget, did you? Robert was using the rustier blade, so I'm going to take you to the hospital, just to be safe.'

Robert appeared at her side in time to catch her last words.

'No.' This time Joshua didn't run. 'Dad's cleaned it for me. He says it's okay.'

'His Dad won't like it if you take him to hospital,' Robert chimed in.

Sister Mary wavered.

'He treats things himself,' Robert added. 'He uses his

own medicine.' He turned to Joshua. 'Come on, Josh, or we'll miss Sister Martha's arithmetic lesson.'

Sister Mary's eyebrows shot up comically at this unusual sign of enthusiasm.

'He'll be all right, Sister. Really.'

Robert pulled him back into the classroom. 'Come on, Josh.'

Joshua went back to sit at his usual place, next to Robert.

CHAPTER THIRTEEN

A cardinal bird darted into the mango tree in search of its mate. Not finding her there, it zoomed out of the tree in a flash of brilliant red and landed on the palm-leaf thatch to look for food. It shoved its beak into the leaves, pecking this way and that, gathering up ants and spiders and swallowing them. It worked its way down the roof, stopping here and there for another tasty morsel, until it came to the edge, where it perched, swaying. Then it dropped down to the window below and balanced there, head to one side.

'Where did you get these?'

Joshua looked round. His father had pulled his box out from under the bed and was holding the four-legged creature in his hand, staring at it, turning it round and round in his strong fingers.

Joshua hadn't noticed him take the broom down from the hook to sweep under the beds. He was cross at not noticing, and even crosser that his father had looked under his bed. 'That's secret, Dad.'

'Ah.' His father looked at him. 'I'm sorry. But since I have seen them, where did you get them, Josh?' His father had stopped turning the little animal. He had found the broken leg and was frowning.

'Outside the hospital. We collected them,' Joshua explained.

'We?'

'Me and Robert. And Millie and Tom and Miriam. You know. Anyway,' he felt less cross now, even quite pleased to be telling his father. 'There was a mountain man in there and he threw them out.'

'Is he still there?' his father asked.

Joshua shook his head. 'He died.'

His father got heavily to his feet, the box in his hands. 'These are rejects, Joshua. The mountain man didn't mean them to be collected. They're broken. That's why he threw them away.'

Joshua crossed the room and took the box from his father and clasped it protectively to him.

'Get rid of them, Josh.' His father's face was set. 'They're bad luck.'

Joshua opened his mouth to argue. He nodded instead.

'Now. Okay?'

Joshua left the house with the box. Once outside, he looked at the two stone carvings. He didn't want to get rid of them. It didn't seem right. But he couldn't keep them under the bed, not any more. Perhaps he could just kind of get rid of them by putting them somewhere else, somewhere outside of the house where he couldn't get to them so easily.

He listened for the steady swish of the broom indoors. His father would be busy for a few minutes yet. He saw a cardinal flit past him towards the shop. That gave him an idea.

He went to the shop, into the back corner where there was a large carton containing paper, string and some old knives his father had discarded but was keeping, just in case. Joshua had never seen him actually look in the carton. Once he put things there he seemed to forget them, and anyway it was Joshua who sorted out the paper. He thought it was rather clever to hide something under his father's nose. *Get rid of them,* he thought, and snorted. He shoved the box down in the bottom of the carton and covered it with the papers and string. The carvings would be safe there. He knocked his elbow on the side as he straightened, and winced. The cut was healing nicely but sometimes it still hurt a bit.

He sneaked back into the house, grabbed a comic from his bed and was out again before his father had a chance to check on him. Pig was outside and he sprawled on the ground, one arm draped over him. Millie had slipped him the comic that afternoon after school. She said her father had been given it by a tourist. Joshua was fascinated by the bright, small pictures.

The words in the bubbles were foreign and he couldn't understand them, but he tried to follow the story through the illustrations. There was a red-headed boy in the first picture with a wicked grin glued to his face; in the second picture he was shaking a tin of something down a friend's shirt. At least, Joshua thought it was a friend, although he didn't look too happy about what was happening.

His father had finished sweeping and was chopping vegetables for the dinner, humming to himself.

Joshua lowered his comic and watched as his father threw the vegetables into the hot oil and added garlic, turmeric and chillies. His head was bare; he must have taken his hat off to sweep under the beds and forgotten to put it on again. Joshua noticed the way the light fell on his hair – straight hair, like his own. He was different to the other men in the village, there was no doubt about that. Joshua had succeeded in shutting out Robert's words, now they came flooding back.

But mountain men who came to this village got sick and died, he reasoned. So his father couldn't be a mountain man, even if his hair was straight. If he was, he wouldn't be here now, alive and well, cooking their meal. There, that proved it.

His father looked up and smiled. 'You're very thoughtful tonight,' he said. 'Didn't you hear me ask for the plates?'

'Oh, sorry. Coming.' He scrambled to his feet and brought them over. 'Dad,' he hesitated. Now that he knew his father wasn't a mountain man, it felt safe to check. Even so, he took a deep breath first. 'Dad, you're not a mountain man, are you?'

His father was startled. 'Who said I was?'

'Well, Robert did.'

'Him again.' He frowned. 'Why?' he went on. 'Would you like me to be a mountain man?'

Joshua shook his head vigorously.

'Well I'm not,' his father said firmly. 'Not so as to count,' Joshua thought he heard him add under his breath.

'Dad?'

His father stood up, frying pan in hand, and looked down at Joshua. 'Where were you born?'

'Here,' Joshua said confidently.

His father nodded. 'And does that make you a boy from the village, or doesn't it?'

Joshua nodded. 'It does.'

'Well then. Now get me my hat, will you?'

Joshua lifted one of Pig's trotters and put the comic under it so it wouldn't blow away, then went inside for his father's hat and swapped it for a plate of food.

That night, lying in bed, he tossed and turned restlessly. He wasn't wholly satisfied by his father's answer. His father had straight hair, he wore a hat, he'd been a butcher, he carved – and there was Pig.

In the morning he went round for Robert. Only Robert's mother was indoors. She always baked on Saturdays, and the room was stiflingly hot from the small iron stove. He hovered hopefully, watching. Perhaps he could double-check with her, he thought. He'd start with the most important question.

'Is my father going to die?' he asked her back, as she bent to open the oven door.

She looked round at him in surprise, then turned back to what she was doing. 'Don't be silly,' she answered at last, taking out a baking sheet and releasing a gush of warm biscuit smell into the air. 'Of course he isn't.' She put a knife under the biscuits to loosen them, then tipped them out one by one on to a piece of raised wire netting to cool.

'Never?' Joshua asked, testing her.

'No, not never. We all have to die one day, my love. But there's no reason he should go just yet, is there?' She looked up in alarm. 'He's not ill, is he?'

'No.' He shook his head.

'Well then. Here,' she handed him one of the hot biscuits and he crammed it into his mouth. Still he lingered by her side.

'Is there something else bothering you?' she asked.

He shook his head, eyes on the ground.

'Robert's going to the market for me,' she said. 'Why

don't you go along with him?'

Just then Robert appeared. 'Mum, Miriam says she won't ... hey, Josh.'

'Go and tell Miriam I want her to help me in here, will you. And ask Tony to look after the others. And make sure Solomon is clean, and – '

Robert escaped, with Joshua on his tail. Sometimes Joshua understood why Robert liked the comparative peace of his home. 'Robert!' they heard his mother shout after them, but Robert didn't stop.

At the market they went straight to Mama Calla.

'You two come to buy or to sell?' she asked.

'Both,' they answered in unison.

'Tell you what, Joshua, you sing for me. Robert, you go and get me a glass of coffee.' She extracted some millis from her pouch and stretched across the piles of fruit to hand them to him.

'Don't you sell berries?' Joshua asked her after he'd settled down beside her.

'Berries?' she asked in surprise. 'No. Plenty of good fruit and vegetables to sell without those. Anyway, *what* berries? None round here. Look, are you going to sing, or aren't you? I don't want you just sitting here chattering. I have a lot of beans that need to be shifted, and tomatoes. Will you sing them first?'

'Fat beans, juicy as ripe tomatoes!' sang Joshua. 'Come buy Mama Calla's beans, sweet as her red tomatoes!'

It didn't go as well as the previous time, perhaps because Mama Calla cramped their style. Robert felt silly copying her phrases while she was there, watching them with narrowed eyes as she drank her coffee. After half an hour she paid them off with a small melon each and a quarter of the price knocked off the vegetables Robert had been sent to buy.

They headed for their usual stretch of wall. Joshua spotted a sharp flat stone near his feet and picked it up. He wiped it on his shorts and dug into his melon, using it as a knife.

'What are you doing?'

'You'll see.' He cut away some melon. 'Here, want this?'

Robert put it in his mouth.

Joshua began whittling at the melon with the stone, but it didn't seem to be working. Pummel came up to them, sniffed at their ankles and barked.

'Here, Pummel, fetch!' Joshua threw the stone for the dog. It looked reproachfully at him and stayed put. Robert found a piece of wood and threw that instead.

Pummel ran, and reached his target just as Swabber came lumbering round the corner towards them.

'Oh-oh.' Joshua put down the melon.

Pummel growled. His legs and back stiffened and he strutted up to Swabber, the piece of wood forgotten. The dogs were sworn enemies. Pummel slowly worked his way around Swabber, sniffing aggressively. Swabber, the older and larger of the dogs, froze, ears flattened against his head. Only his eyeballs moved, rolling back in his head. Pummel nipped him experimentally on his hind leg.

That was enough. Swabber leaped round on all fours to face Pummel, snarling, lips drawn high over his gums.

A couple of men had gathered. Now more sauntered over as the dogs began to circle each other. Pummel pounced and drew blood. Swabber's hackles rose. Still he snarled.

'Two korias on Swabber!' a man yelled. There was mocking laughter from the onlookers.

'Make it five for Pummel!' called out another.

Joshua and Robert went over and joined the men who were forming a rough circle around the dogs.

The stakes climbed to eight korias. Swabber and Pummel, sensing the atmosphere, flew at each other in earnest. Pummel was smaller and sharper. When Swabber pinned him down and lowered his head to bite, he wriggled free, and raced around the older dog.

There was ragged cheering from the crowd.

Swabber turned, trying to keep pace with Pummel, trying to make sure he was always facing him. Pummel launched himself at the side Swabber least expected, bit, drew blood and darted away again before Swabber was able to retaliate. He came in again. This time Swabber managed to graze him with his teeth, but not before Pummel had sunk his deep into Swabber's leg. Swabber let out a howl.

The men surrounding them grew silent, intent on the fighting. Not even the man who had placed a bet on Swabber was egging him on now.

Joshua's heart thudded. He tried to swallow but his mouth was dry. Dogfights were common in the village, but he didn't really want to watch this. He was sure that Swabber was going to be slaughtered.

Pummel threw himself at Swabber's head. He seized an ear in his sharp teeth and tugged hard. Swabber howled again.

Suddenly a hand grabbed the back of Joshua's shirt and jerked him to his feet. His father broke through the circle of men and threw the sack he'd been carrying over Pummel's head.

At once the snarling turned to a whine. Mutters rose from the spectators. Joshua's father ignored them.

'Go!' he ordered Swabber.

Swabber didn't move. He seemed stunned.

'Go!' He pushed the dog with his foot. Swabber shook himself and slunk off, limping.

'Who asked you to interfere? Get out of here! Meatseller!' a man hurled the curse at Joshua's father.

'He's not!' Joshua shouted.

But his father didn't answer. He took the sack off Pummel's head. 'Joshua! Robert!' he called.

The boys went over, trying not to look at the men. Pummel barked and wagged his tail, transformed in a second from a vicious fighting dog to the playful mongrel they knew. Joshua bent down to pat him. He couldn't help himself.

When he straightened up, Simon was standing in front of his father.

'Come on, you two,' his father said in a quiet voice, stepping to the left to avoid Simon. Simon stepped to the left too. He moved to the right, but again Simon blocked his way.

'Hello, Simon,' Joshua said, edging closer to his father.

Simon took no notice. He was staring hard at Joshua's father. For a moment no sound came through the damaged teeth. Then, 'Meatseller!' spurted out on a wave of rotting breath.

Joshua's father flinched. He put out his hand for Joshua, and Joshua took it. He gave his other hand to Robert, but Robert pretended he hadn't seen. Then he turned away, brushing past Simon.

'Meatseller!' Simon swore again. He threw back his head, arched and then spat at their feet.

Deliberately, Joshua stepped on the glistening glob, covering it from his father's eyes. He ground it into the earth, staring straight ahead, trying not to retch at the slipperiness under his skin. The three of them walked through the circle of men, restless now and breaking up as the men drifted away.

As they walked off, they could hear Simon cackling maliciously, but no one else tried to interfere with them.

Joshua's father squeezed his hand reassuringly and then let go. Once they were beyond the market area he stopped and slumped against a wall, his eyes screwed tight. For a long moment he just rested there, saying nothing. Then he squared his shoulders and opened his eyes. 'We couldn't have Swabber being beaten, now could we, boys?'

Joshua was astonished to see him wink.

'That wasn't a fair fight; Swabber is too old and slow for a young pup like Pummel.'

Not a word about what had happened after.

But Joshua would not let the insult go so easily. 'You don't even sell meat any more!' he cried indignantly, still trembling from the ugly scene.

'That's right,' his father agreed. He wiped his arm across his damp forehead but beads of perspiration sprang up again as soon as he had done so. 'Don't let them get to you, Josh. Not ever. Now,' he went on, pushing himself away from the wall. 'I was going for a walk. Why don't you both come with me?'

Since the day of the riot he hadn't carved, and since he'd started smoking fish he rarely drank. He went for walks more and more often. He was restless, always on the move.

'Where are we going?' Robert asked as they rounded the hospital.

'Round the back here,' Joshua's father answered, heading for the trees.

'Oh.' Robert stopped dead. He was silent for a moment. 'I think I'll see what's going on at the Gola,' he said to Joshua.

Joshua's father noticed Joshua dithering. 'Go with Robert if you want to.'

They split up and went in different directions, Robert and Joshua towards the hotel and the jetty.

After a few steps, Joshua turned and looked back, uneasily remembering the sweat on his father's forehead. It reminded him of someone else, but he couldn't think who. Behind the banks of oleander bushes that surrounded the hospital were other, taller bushes with dark glossy leaves. Behind that, trees grew thickly, seeming to merge into the darkness of the high, looming mountains which shut out the sky and the sun. There was no path there. And there was no sign of his father. He'd been swallowed up by the darkness.

Robert came and stood at his side. 'That's the way the mountain men take when they come to the coast.'

Joshua looked at his friend, his unease returning.

'Oh, come *on*,' Robert said. 'I'm not saying your father's one of them. Only that that's the way the men from the mountain go.'

CHAPTER FOURTEEN

In the shadows Swabber skulked, tail half raised. His wounds had healed and he was hungry. He licked his lips, staring into the pool of light. The smell of fried fish filled the air. He raised his muzzle and whined.

Joshua looked up from his eating. His father was watching him, as intently as a cat might a mouse, with an odd look on his face. His plate was full but he hadn't touched his food.

'What is it, Dad?'

'Nothing,' his father answered.

Joshua went back to his supper, spooning up a bit of rice here, a bit of mackerel there, some beans. The clinking of his spoon against the enamel plate sounded loud in the stillness. The last morsel was on its way to his mouth when he saw a spasm cross his father's face.

'Dad? 'Are you all right, Dad?'

'Yes.' But his father's voice was strained, tinged with pain. He pushed the untouched plate from him and it fell to the ground.

Swabber whined and crept forward.

'Dad?' Joshua stood up in alarm.

The dog flattened himself on the ground.

His father waved one arm in the air in an attempt at reassurance. 'Not hungry,' he said. 'Feel a bit sick. It'll pass.' With that a grimace shot across his face. He folded his arms across his stomach and rocked backward and forward, groaning.

Joshua was at his side. 'What can I do? Will I call someone? Mama Siska?'

'No, no. I'll be all right in the morning. Just help me to bed, there's a good boy.'

Joshua looped his father's arm over his shoulders and helped him to his feet. Together they staggered up the steps, his father leaning heavily on him.

Behind them, Swabber edged towards the plate. He sniffed it once, then wolfed everything down, licking the plate clean before he limped back into the shadows.

Joshua's father got into bed fully dressed. 'I'm cold,' he said, shivering. 'Make me some tea, will you, Joshua? ' He groaned as another stab of pain hit him. 'Tea,' he repeated.

Joshua half filled the kettle and lit the spirit heater. He squatted beside it, willing it to boil quickly, his heart pounding. 'Let him be all right,' he found himself praying with all his might. 'Oh God, let Dad be all right.'

When he went back in with the tea he took the cotton cover from his own bed and put it over his father's and sat with him while he drank the hot liquid.

His father smiled wanly at him. 'I'll be fine, Josh.' He patted his hand. 'You go to bed. Go to sleep. Goodnight.' He pulled Joshua to him and kissed him on the forehead.

'Goodnight, Dad,' Joshua said, subdued. He lay down on his bed, still in his clothes. He decided to stay awake all night in case his father needed him. But after a short while he fell into a deep sleep. He woke in the middle of the night to the barking of a dog, the sour smell of vomit and the sound of his father's moans.

He scrambled up. His father was half in bed, half on the floor. Somehow he managed to push him back in. His father was muttering something. 'What? What did you say? Dad?' Joshua bent closer to listen. 'What?' He shook his father gently. He didn't understand the words; they sounded like another language. And his father no longer seemed to recognise him.

Joshua went back to his own bed and sat on the edge, not sure what to do. He got up and stood over his father. 'I'm going for Robert's mother,' he said.

His father didn't react. Joshua felt panic rising. He tore down the steps, across the clearing and up the steps to Robert's house. He burst into the room, gasping, 'Help! Please come! Dad's sick. He can't talk to me. Oh, please ...'

Almost immediately Robert's mother was at his side,

pulling a dress over her head. 'What's this?'

He began to cry. She gripped him tightly. 'Josh, what is it?'

'Dad's ill.' he gulped. 'I'm scared.'

Robert appeared and stood close to Joshua. Now the entire family was awake; in the background a baby cried and another voice soothed it. Leon joined them.

Robert's mother had taken charge. 'Robert, go and fetch old Mama Siska.' she ordered. 'Quick.'

Robert was out and away.

'Now, Joshua, come with me. Leon, will you come?' She raised her voice. 'Miriam, look after the baby.'

'You stay here.' Leon spoke to Solomon, who was gazing at Joshua with enormous sleep-filled eyes, his thumb glued to his mouth.

Joshua reached his father's bed first. There was no change. He stood aside for her. 'I don't understand what he's saying,' he said.

'They're not words I know,' Robert's mother said, listening. She looked askance at him. 'Maybe they're mountain words.'

He stared at her. What if he was wrong after all? What if his father really was a mountain man? 'Will he be okay?'

'Where *is* Mama Siska?' she asked, not answering.

'Here I am.' The old lady shuffled into the house. She looked once, piercingly, at Joshua. 'Go and stand with

Robert at the door,' she ordered. He backed off as she bent over the figure in the bed.

After that everything happened very quickly. From the doorway he watched old Mama Siska prodding and talking, and saw her head nod at some suggestion of Leon's. Leon pushed past them and Joshua didn't dare ask where he was going. He came back with three other men. One was Simon. Joshua rushed over to his father and stood with his back to him, protecting him. 'No!' he cried. 'You can't take him!'

'Don't be silly, Josh,' Robert's mother said. 'Let them get him out of bed.'

'Yes. Hospital's the best place. They'll know what to do with him there.'

Joshua squirmed out from under their arms and blocked them. 'Mama Siska!' he appealed.

'Simon's right,' she said gently. 'It is your father's only chance.' But she avoided his eyes.

'No-ooo.' he howled, and head-butted a man who was approaching the bed.

The man batted him aside like a wasp.

Leon held him. 'Listen, Joshua – '

'No! You can't take him to the hospital, you can't.'

'He'll get care there.' Another voice. Another pair of hands.

'No!' He bit the hand that was restraining him and it fell from his shoulders, the owner cursing. Joshua kicked and struggled. He had to save his father.

But it was no use. The men had his father now and were already bearing him from the room. He couldn't fight any more. They didn't understand. His despair turned to grief and he ran to Robert's mother, crying.

'He'll be lonely. He'll die,' he sobbed, 'I know he'll die.'

She held him close and led him back to his bed. He closed his eyes. What would happen to him if his father died? Robert and Milllie and Tom had uncles and aunts and cousins. All he had was his father.

Robert's mother stroked his cheek gently. He was glad she was there. Maybe he could go to live with Robert and her and their family. She had so many children; maybe there'd be room for just one more, he thought. 'Don't let Dad die,' he prayed silently, 'don't let him.'

He felt her draw the cover up to his chin. She stayed with him till she thought he was asleep, but he was only pretending. There was a cold, heavy lump inside him that made him think he would never sleep again. After she left he rolled himself into a tight ball and prayed even harder.

When he opened his eyes again it was morning and Robert's mother was back. Joshua sat up in bed and scanned her face anxiously. What news was she bringing?

She sat on his bed and held out her arms to him. 'He died on the operating table, Josh. It was too late,' she said.

Mountain man, he thought miserably. So his father really had been a mountain man. He should have stopped them. No mountain man came out of the hospital alive.

Joshua sat on the top step of his house, head down, his chin in his hands, a plate of food at his side. Behind him, in the clearing, Robert's mother approached, the younger children bobbing in her wake like ducklings. When she reached the shop she stopped, turned and shooed them away.

She was at the bottom step before Joshua noticed her. He smiled wanly.

She hugged him and he started to cry again. She held him close and rocked him till he grew calmer. 'Couldn't you eat your breakfast?' She'd made it for him earlier before going off to look after her family.

He shook his head. 'I'm not hungry.'

'No? Well.' She got to her feet and put out a hand to him. 'Come on, let's make some coffee. Show me where the things are kept. Come on, love.'

He took down the jars of coffee and sugar from the shelf, the spoons, his mug, then his father's. She lit the stove outside. He brought water in the kettle and put it on to boil. The familiar movements were comforting.

'Make enough for three,' she said, bringing out the

spare mug. 'Sister Martha is joining us.'

By the time the water was boiled, Sister Martha had arrived. Joshua handed the women their coffee and sat on the step between them, nursing his mug. For a while no one spoke.

'What's going to happen to me?' he burst out finally, turning to Robert's mother. 'Can I come and live with you?'

She opened her mouth but it was Sister Martha who answered first. 'You're going to come to us,' she said.

His head swivelled round to her.

'At the convent,' she went on. She was smiling gently. 'We'll take care of you.'

'With the orphans?'

'Yes,' she answered briskly. 'Would you like that?'

He turned back to Robert's mother. 'Am I an orphan?' he appealed to her.

'Yes,' she answered.

He digested that.

'Why can't I come and live with you?'

'We haven't got room for another, my love. But you can come round and see us as often as you like.'

Sister Martha put her hand gently on his arm. One short hair on her forehead had escaped the tight white band of her headdress and was fluttering in the air. She was smiling. Joshua decided that he liked Sister Martha. 'Can Pig come too?' he asked.

'Of course he can.' She put down the tin mug. 'Now, I have to go back. I've got things to do. I'll see you soon, all right? Come when you're ready.' She leaned over and kissed him on the top of his head, then went down the steps and left them.

Robert's mother sighed, then smiled brightly at Joshua. 'You'll be fine,' she reassured him. 'Come on now. Let's get your things together for the convent.'

He trailed inside after her. He didn't have much: his rattles, his book of fruit, his spare pair of shorts and a shirt, a tatty vest, his enamel plate and mug.

When she asked if she could have the other plate and mug – his father's – Joshua nodded dumbly, and said that she could have the spare mug and the good glasses too, and anything else she wanted. But he took his father's best shirt and his cracked leather belt.

'Then I'll give Leon his shorts,' she said, 'they're far too big for you.' He knew they were, and he nodded again.

They took the sheets and pillow cases off the beds and used one of the pillow cases to put his things in.

'And Pig,' Joshua said. Pig was in his usual nighttime place at the door, his back shiny from being leant against and stroked.

Joshua took hold of one leg and pulled Pig out of the doorway and on to the top step. *Bump*. Another bump, and he was on the ground.

'Hold on.' She took hold of another leg. They carried the wooden animal awkwardly across the clearing.

Robert and Millie ran up. 'I have a job for you two,' she said. 'Help Joshua take his stuff to the convent, and then come back here. I'll make some chocolatey biscuits, the ones you like so much, as a treat. Sister Martha will let you come too,' she added, seeing Joshua's face fall again. 'Tell her I asked you.'

Joshua woke up drowsily to the sound of water slapping on stone and a light breeze across his face. For a moment he had a fantasy that he was in the bedroom with the balcony at the Gola hotel, but when he opened his eyes and saw another bed next to his and one beyond that, he remembered. It was his second morning waking in this bed. He closed his eyes again. He and the six other orphans slept together in a dormitory beyond the nuns' quarters, at the tip of the L-shaped building. One side of the room was open – just like the classrooms – and an open-air corridor ran alongside it. There were glass sliding doors, but Marius, who slept in the next bed, had shown Joshua the rusty runners and told him that the doors were never pulled closed. When the rains came, the beds on that side were simply pushed into the middle of the room.

Between the convent and the classrooms was the school playground, and beyond that lay the sea. The sound he heard had been the sea hitting against the sea wall. High tide, he thought.

He didn't mind being in the orphanage. It was safe. He liked having his own locker at the side of the bed. He'd put his clothes in it and his book. Pig spent the night within reach too, in front of the locker door, and in the daytime he guarded the foot of the bed. Joshua planned to go back and pick up the carvings – he hadn't wanted to when Robert's mother was there – so that he could put them in the locker as well.

Marius snuffled in his sleep and Joshua turned over. Vincent was on the other side; he was only four, and all you could see of him was the top of his head peeping out from under the sheet. The three girls were in the row on the far side of the room. Catherine, Marius's older sister, lay sprawled out on top of the sheet. She said she preferred it that way. Joshua was the oldest of all the orphans. Out of school hours he could play with his old friends, Sister Martha had said; they didn't have to be from the convent. No harm, she said. Anyway, they had two weeks' holiday now.

In some ways, life wasn't so different from before, Joshua thought. Except that he misssed his father so much. It was strange not to hear his father's snores and grunts from the other side of the room, not to hear the rustling of insects and lizards in the palm leaves above their heads. Memories of the night his father had died came rushing into his head.

Perhaps if he hadn't kept the carvings his father would not have died. Or – he thought back further – maybe if Father Peter hadn't forgotten to bless the front of the shop none of the trouble with Pig would have started, and his father wouldn't have become ill.

No, it wasn't that, he thought miserably, punching a fist into his pillow; it was the carvings. His father had told him quite clearly to throw away the carvings and he hadn't. That would have been important if his father was a mountain man. It was all his fault.

He burrowed into his pillow.

'Up, Joshua! Come on now!'

Sister Martha. He opened his eyes. He must have fallen asleep again. The others were up and waiting for him. He scrambled out and stood beside his bed.

'Ready, sleepyhead?' Sister Martha asked.

He joined his hands together and closed his eyes.

'God bless to us this day,' she said.

'And ourselves to His service, Amen.' They all replied in unison.

'Breakfast in ten minutes. Hurry up now.'

There were three wash basins at the end of the dormitory, with running water, and lavatories that flushed. Joshua put the plug in one of the basins and wet his face half-heartedly. After breakfast, he resolved, he would go back to the shop and pick up the carvings.

'Move over.' Marius nudged him. 'It's my turn.'

Joshua grinned wickedly and hit the water with the flat of his hand, spraying Marius, who splashed back, even harder.

'Hey!' Catherine protested from the next basin along as the water hit her. She cupped her hands in her basin and sloshed back, just at the same time as Joshua. They both caught Marius.

Marius didn't think it was funny any more. Joshua and Catherine ran headlong out of the room, giggling, with Marius in chase. At the bottom of the stairs Sister Mary was waiting. 'Is that the way to come downstairs?' she chided them as they landed at her feet in a tumble. 'Good morning,' she greeted them.

They straightened themselves quickly. 'Good morning, Sister Mary,' they chorused and fell in behind her, walking sedately to the refectory.

After breakfast Joshua went back to his house. As he jumped up the steps a sudden hope flared in his heart – perhaps his father would be there?

He wasn't, of course. Joshua stood in the middle of the room, taking in the scene: the beds with no sheets, the bare shelf, the single rickety chair. Someone had taken down the cotton curtain over the door. The place looked empty, unlived-in. He swallowed to fight the lump in his throat and blinked hard. It was home no more.

He trudged round to the shop, mechanically reaching out to pull aside the fishnet curtain. That too had been removed.

Nothing else had been touched. A knife lay rusting on the table where his father had left it, and there were still a couple of fish beneath the counter.

'Whew!' Joshua pinched his nostrils tight. The fish stank. He went to the carton at the back of the shop and looked in. The box with the carvings was still there! He lifted it out and set it down on the corner of the chopping table. He took out the snake and the four-legged creature, pulled his shirt out of his shorts and used the bottom of it to polish them. When he was satisfied, he put them back in the box, picked it up and looked around.

He spotted the crocheted cover that old Mama Siska had said his mother had made. He reached in over the smelly fish and plucked it out. He stuffed it in his pocket and left. He didn't look back.

Millie and Tom materialised out of nowhere. Then Robert, and Solomon and Miriam. It was as if they'd been waiting for him. But Joshua didn't want to be distracted, and he went on walking. Robert and Millie and Tom fell into step with him, and the other two tagged on behind.

'Where are you taking that?' Robert asked, noticing the box.

'He's taking it to the convent, silly,' Millie said. 'We'll come with you, shall we, Josh? Then we can play.'

Joshua stopped suddenly. Solomon bumped into him, and was about to wail when Robert glared at him. He stifled the cry, and had to make do with looking sulky.

Joshua had remembered what his father said about the carvings. He couldn't take them to the convent, he thought unhappily. But where *could* he go? What else could he do with them? He started walking again, in the direction of the convent, but unsure of his final destination.

Their path took them along the sea front. When they reached the harbour, Joshua hesitated. Perhaps this was the answer. He turned down the track that led out to the jetty. Robert followed. The others dropped behind, losing interest, and began playing in the sand.

Joshua carried the box with its precious load to the end of the jetty, where the water was deep. Seaweed had come in on the tide and was trapped against the wooden pier. The weed smelled powerful and fishy in the hot sun and the water heaved under its weight.

Joshua stood looking out to sea, unmoving.

'Why are we here, Josh?' Robert said at last, breaking the silence. 'Let's go back.'

'You go,' Joshua said, looking at Robert, but not seeing him properly because there was a film of tears over his eyes.

'I'm staying,' retorted Robert, noticing the unshed tears. He didn't want to leave Joshua like this.

Joshua began to take the animals out of the box.

'What are you going to do with those?' Robert asked. He remembered that Joshua had no home any more, nowhere to keep private things. 'Let me look after them,' he offered. He held out his hands.

Joshua handed him the empty box.

'I didn't mean that,' Robert protested.

'I know you didn't.' A tear trickled down Joshua's cheek. He held a carving in each hand and turned to face the open sea. He lifted the snake over his head and hissed, as if he was the snake himself.

'Don't!' Robert cried, suddenly realising what Joshua was about to do.

Too late. The snake left Joshua's hand. It rose in the air and spun a little, catching the sun. Then it fell, hitting the seaweed with a plop before dropping through to the water below. The seaweed closed over the hole.

Robert was stunned. He grabbed Joshua's arm, the one holding the four-legged creature.

'No! 'I have to do it!' Joshua cried, tears streaming down his face. 'Dad told me to get rid of them, and I never did, so he died! Don't you see?'

Robert let go. The four-legged creature fell through the air and landed on its back on the seaweed, its three good legs pointing skywards. A hole gaped, the seaweed heaved, and it too was gone; there was nothing to show where it had been.

They both stood, staring into the water. Joshua wiped the back of his hand over his face.

Robert, bewildered, was the first to turn away. Joshua watched him walk down the jetty, saw him speak to the others, then they scattered and went off, leaving him alone.

It was what he had wanted. Just the same, he wished they hadn't gone.

Back at the convent he found Marius and Vincent and Catherine in a huddle in the playground. He went over to join them. Catherine looked up. 'Go away,' she told him.

'Why?' He peered over their shoulders, trying to see what it was they had on the ground. He circled round till he was behind Marius. 'Let me in,' he wheedled.

Marius looked back at him over his shoulder. 'No,' he said, shuffling closer to the others, closing a gap.

Joshua was taken aback. 'Why not?'

'Because this is to do with us. *You* wouldn't understand,' Catherine answered.

Joshua felt his face go hot. He turned and ran to the dormitory, grabbed hold of Pig and dragged him to the corner of the room furthest from the playground. He sat on the floor beside Pig and rested his aching head on the broad back. He could smell the oil in the wood. He closed his eyes.

'Josh?' He opened his eyes. Sister Martha was squatting beside him.

He smiled at her.

'Are you all right?'

He nodded. He didn't know how long he'd been asleep.

'Sure?'

He was, now. He felt fine.

'Good.' She got up. 'In that case, outside with you. Go and find the others.'

He stood up. Sister Martha picked up Pig's front legs. 'Come on, I'll help you take him back to your bed. And now, shoo. Go on, out you go.'

When he went outside, the others had disappeared. He didn't want to go looking for them, not yet, they might ignore him again. Instead he wandered back to the shop. He trailed his fingers along the counter and on along the table till they came to the knife. He hesitated. His fingers moved towards it. He picked it up. The wooden handle rested easily in the palm of his hand. It was the knife his father had used to carve with.

He took it outside to the standpipe. He turned on the tap and let water stream on to the stone underneath.

When he thought the stone was wet enough, he began sharpening the knife on it – back and forth in long strokes – till the edge showed clean and shiny. He hunted around the yard for a piece of wood but couldn't find any he liked.

He went to the beach. No one was around; it was too early for the fishermen and their dragnet. The tideline was marked by a line of brown seaweed that had been abandoned by the receding waters. He walked along with his eyes down, looking for a suitable bit of driftwood, stamping on the seaweed bubbles to make them pop. He bent to pick up a long, forked strand, and there, beneath it, saw a promising piece of dark wood. He brought it a little way up the beach, sat down and began to whittle. It was a good feeling, rough wood, hot from the sun, in one hand, and the smooth knife handle in the other. Chips flew into the air and landed on his legs, tickling them.

'Joshua!'

He looked up. Marius was running down the beach towards him. 'Sister Martha says, do you want a drink?'

On the path behind Marius he saw the figure of the nun. He was surprised; he hadn't realised that his wanderings had taken him so close to the convent.

As he got up, he slipped the knife underneath the wood so that it wouldn't show. He wasn't sure that knives would be allowed in their lockers.

'Sister, Joshua was carving,' Marius announced. 'Look.'

Joshua half held out the wood then pulled it back. 'I haven't finished it.'

'You're not really from here, are you?' Marius stated matter-of-factly.

'Of course he is,' Sister Martha corrected him sharply.

But Joshua felt uncomfortable under Marius's stare.

CHAPTER SIXTEEN

In the rubbish heap, the discarded skin of a melon heaved as two rats fought over it, squeaking loudly, dislodging rotting fruit and tin cans. One rolled down the heap and landed right at Joshua's feet as he walked past. Robert hadn't been at home when he'd called, nor Tom nor Millie. The tin was a welcome distraction. He kicked it away from the pile and dribbled it like a football, swerving to one side of the road and then to the other. He knocked it into an imaginary goal and raised his arms in the air in triumph.

A car hooted. He jumped and turned round. Cars were a rare sight in the village. This one had gleaming red paintwork and its engine purred like a well-fed cat. Joshua could see his face in its shiny bonnet. He reached out to stroke it.

'Boo!' Millie jumped out.

'Millie!' He stared at her and at the open door. 'Were you in the car?'

She nodded, beaming with excitement. 'Come on,' she said, pulling at his arm. 'It's the tourists. They want you too.'

He scrambled into the back seat. The nearest he had ever got to riding in a car was a ramshackle old lorry used as a bus. He reached over and pulled the door shut.

The woman in the passenger seat turned round and smiled at him.

'Isn't it great, Josh?' Millie was burbling. 'They're taking us to the Gola.' She looked uncertain for a moment. 'At least, I think that's what they were saying. When I saw you I told them to stop. Aren't you glad, hey?' She punched him playfully.

Joshua punched her back and she giggled.

'All right, Marguerite?' The man in the driver's seat patted the woman's knee and let off the handbrake.

Marguerite? Joshua looked closely at the couple, recognising the strange name. It was the same pair he'd met when he had carried their package from the craft shop.

The woman twisted in her seat again and looked at him. 'Yoswa?' she asked.

He nodded, more interested in the car than in her. The leather seat was hot under his thighs and it stuck to his bare skin. When he shifted, it released him with a soft, sucking sound. The smell was strong too: leather and petrol and metal all blended together.

He listened to the car engine throb as they moved off and hunched forward to watch the dials turning slowly on the dashboard as the man drove, not wanting to miss a second of it.

Millie turned round and knelt on the seat to look through the back window. After a while, Joshua joined her, but there wasn't much to see: only swirling clouds of sand churned up in the wake of the car. The dials were far more interesting.

The car drew up outside the hotel.

'You can get out now,' the man said, gesturing, leaning back and opening Millie's door.

'Come on.' The woman beckoned them to follow her as she headed for one of the tables outside the bar.

Millie flounced after them as if it was the most natural thing in the world. Joshua held back.

'What are you doing here?' Oliver asked, appearing suddenly on the path beside him.

'I'm with them,' Joshua said doubtfully.

'Pull the other one,' Oliver laughed.

Joshua scowled and ran after the others. He pulled out a chair and slid on to it, leaving Oliver gawping.

Drinks were set before them.

'We shouldn't be here,' Joshua said to Millie, uneasily aware of the disapproving glint in the barman's eye.

'Why shouldn't we?' retorted Millie, her chin jutting out. She smoothed her dress down over her knees and placed one hand over the stain on the skirt. She leaned forward and took a delicate sip from her glass.

Joshua nursed his glass in his hands as the woman was doing. The cold drink chilled his fingers and little rivulets of condensation ran down the sides of the glass. He stared down at it, not sure what to say now they were here. Even Millie had subsided into silence.

The man and woman exchanged few words too; they seemed content to observe the children.

The woman reached down for her handbag. From it she took an envelope and produced photographs which she spread out on the table in front of them. They showed a tall brick house with windows with glass in them that gleamed and looked at you like so many eyes.

She pointed to herself and the man and then at the house. 'We live here,' she said.

Millie and Joshua nodded, eyes wide.

'This is our bedroom.' She put her hands together at one side and rested her head on them, pretending to snore.

'Bedroom.' Joshua tried to repeat the foreign word.

The woman looked delighted. 'Yes,' she said, 'bedroom. Here's another bedroom.'

It was painted blue and green and had one bed in it. Joshua stared. He picked up the photograph. There was a window and, outside it, the top of a tree. So the room was very high up, he thought wonderingly. Beyond the tree was a sloping red roof, not thatched like theirs, or made of concrete. The floor was covered in blue and there were high wooden head and tailboards to the bed, as high as on Old Mama Siska's ancient bed which he'd once seen through the window, and a curving side which made it look like a boat. He saw books on the shelves, a bunch of flowers, and a clock on the windowsill. He gazed greedily at it, imagining himself in that bed, pretending the room was all his.

Millie nudged him. 'Look,' she said, awe written all over her face, 'this is where they cook and eat, and this is another room.' He saw the kitchen and the drawing-room, large places full of strange things. 'What a big house,' she breathed. 'It's like a hotel.'

Joshua noticed her smile extra sweetly at the woman when she was asked if she'd like another drink.

'Where do you live?' the man asked, pointing at Millie and then at Joshua.

'At home,' Millie said, 'in Botelo.'

The man clearly understood the name of the village.

'At the convent,' Joshua said in turn.

This time the man looked puzzled, not recognising the word.

Joshua mimed a nun's habit and put his hands together in prayer. Millie giggled.

'Oh.' The man's face cleared. 'The orphanage.' He examined him with interest.

'Orphanage,' Joshua repeated, getting his tongue round the strange word.

'You see? I said he was bright that first time, remember?' the woman said to the man, the foreign words tumbling from her lips. 'And what a stroke of luck that he's an orphan! You don't think – after all these years hoping ... ' she sighed wistfully, leaving the words hanging in the air.

'Oddly enough,' the man said, 'I thought I recognised his name when Reverend Mother discussed the children with us.'

They gazed thoughtfully at each other.

'What are they saying, Josh?' Millie asked.

'How should I know?' he retorted. He fidgeted under the strangers' stare and picked up the photograph of the bedroom again.

The woman took off her sunglasses. 'Would you like to sleep in that bedroom?' she asked, pointing at Joshua and the bedroom, and again mimicking sleep.

'Don't rush him, dear,' the man said, laying his hand on hers. 'One step at a time.'

Joshua looked from one to the other, bewildered by what he thought the woman had meant. Millie, feeling ignored, began to pout. 'Come on, Josh, let's go.' She got down from the chair. 'Well, are you coming?'

He left his chair reluctantly, flashed a smile over his shoulder and followed Millie.

CHAPTER SEVENTEEN

A lizard fell off the wall, landed on the ground and waited, absolutely still, checking that no one or nothing had noticed. Satisfied, it scurried into the shade at the base of the wall, its tail weaving to keep up with its tiny strong feet. A large splinter of wood blocked its path. The lizard's tongue flickered. It went round the obstacle and continued along. Another chipping fell, right in front of the lizard. It froze.

'Joshua!'

Joshua dropped the piece of driftwood and the whittling knife over the far side of the wall, just missing the lizard. 'Yes, Sister?'

'Father Peter wants you to serve at Mass,' Sister Martha said, whisking him off to the chapel to find a surplice that fitted.

'Can't I sing?' Joshua asked plaintively. 'I'd rather sing.' He quite enjoyed his short solos, even if Robert did tease him afterwards.

'Not today. Today's your turn to serve.' Only the orphans served at school Mass. It was their privilege.

'But I've never done it before.'

'There's always a first time,' she said, taking down the starched cotton garment from the shelf.

'I don't know what to do.'

The nun looked at him in mock fury. 'And how many times have you been to Mass, young man?' she scolded. 'Of course you know what to do.' She pulled the white surplice down over his head, plucking at its folds to get it to hang right. 'Anyway, I'll be nearby in case you need me.'

Joshua wriggled inside the surplice. The white sleeves fell below his elbows and felt awkward, and the starched cloth itched at his neck. But once the school came filing in and silence fell in the chapel and the Mass began, he forgot the discomfort. He became caught up in the prayers and the words, in the light and burning wax from the tall candles banked high on the altar, and he remembered at which point he had to kneel and stand and bow.

'Lift up your hearts,' the priest intoned.

'We lift them up to the Lord,' he responded along with the others. He had the brass bell in his hand and watched the priest, concentrating. Father Peter spread his hands over the holy wine in the chalice and Joshua rang the bell, once, twice.

As he filed out behind the priest at the end of Mass he glanced at Sister Martha and she nodded her approval. He cast down his eyes and tried to look solemn going down the aisle. At the last row of seats his eyes fell on two pairs of large feet in shoes, one with laces, the other high and strapped, with painted toenails peeping through. He gazed up from the feet in astonishment. It was the tourist couple again. The woman smiled warmly at him and he smiled back. Then, remembering himself, he bowed his head once more and followed the priest into the vestry to disrobe.

When he came out they were gone. In a few minutes, lessons would start. He ran out to the playground and retrieved his knife and the wood from behind the wall. He looked around for a better hiding place.

'What are those?'

He jumped. He hadn't heard Robert approach.

He put the knife behind his back.

'Let's see,' Robert coaxed.

'No. It's secret,' Joshua said stiffly.

The bell for lessons clanged, distracting Joshua. Robert grabbed the wood and knife from him.

Joshua didn't try to take them back. There didn't seem much point. His hands dangled at his side.

Robert examined the piece of wood. He ran a finger over the head that was beginning to appear and down over the back that Joshua had rounded and smoothed. 'Oh,' he said tonelessly. He stared at Joshua, then held out the wood and knife. 'Here.'

Joshua took them.

Their eyes locked. Robert was the first to look away. 'Hide them,' he said, his voice cool and distant. 'Don't let the others know you're carving. Try under that stone over there.' He turned on his heel.

Joshua hurried over to the stone and lifted it. There was a hollow in the ground beneath. He put the wood and knife in there, replaced the stone and ran to catch up with Robert.

Robert didn't grin at him as usual. He didn't even turn his head. He quickened his pace.

So did Joshua.

Robert headed down the aisle for their desk, Joshua hard on his heels.

'Joshua!'

He stopped. Sister Mary was beckoning him. 'I asked you to sit over here, remember?' She pointed to the empty desk in front.

'But that was last week, Sister,' he pleaded. Robert had sat down at their desk.

'And this is this week. You've come in late without a word of apology or explanation, and I want you in this desk.'

'That's not fair!' Joshua said. Robert had come in late too.

'Don't answer back! Go to the desk at once.'

He went. When the nun turned to the blackboard to write down the names of world capitals, he looked round. Robert was holding a whispered conversation across the aisle and he was unable to get his attention, though he tried. He sighed, opened his exercise book and began copying the names off the board.

Robert would think he was a mountain boy because of the carving. He had to talk to him. Again he looked round. Robert was writing, head down.

He turned back to his book. New Delhi, he copied down, Jakarta, Islamabad, Maputo. A film of tears clouded his eyes, blurring the words on the blackboard. He blinked, and wrote: Canberra, Amsterdam, Rome, Nairobi.

A tear overflowed and dropped on to the last *i*. He wiped it with his fist, smudging it. London, Dublin, Tokyo, Bangkok, he went on.

Tears dripped silently down on to the page. The lead of his pencil slid off the wetness.

There was a hand on his shoulder. 'Here.' Sister Mary passed him her handkerchief. 'Blow your nose. It isn't as bad as that.'

Yes it is, he thought, blowing into it. He remembered Robert saying that no one wanted to be friends with his father. Perhaps Robert would stop being his friend now that he'd seen him carve. Marius had already told some of the others; he could tell from the glances they gave him. He held the handkerchief out to Sister Mary.

'Keep it,' she said, patting him. 'Now,' she raised her

voice to the class, 'who is going to tell me which country's capital cities these are? Yes, Rosemarie, which is the first?'

'India,' Rosemarie said.

'Good girl.' She chalked India up next to New Delhi.

'And Jakarta?'

Joshua looked round again. This time Robert's head was up. He was staring at the blackboard. Joshua could not catch his eye. 'Robert!' he mouthed.

It was no good.

He turned back to his work. Dully he wrote down India, Indonesia, Pakistan, Mozambique, in turn. He felt desolate.

'Australia,' someone called out.

'Netherlands.'

He knew only half the places.

'Excuse me, Sister.' Sister Martha came in and went over to Sister Mary. They talked quietly, their covered heads close together like two white birds, the starched cotton quivering. Sister Martha seemed to be explaining something. Sister Mary looked across at Joshua. Behind him he could hear restless shuffling and whispering. He sat there miserably, his mind a blank.

He saw Sister Mary nod. Sister Martha came over to his desk. 'Put away your book, Joshua,' she said. 'Reverend Mother wants you in her study.'

His stomach plummeted. You only went to Reverend

Mother when you had done something really wrong.

'There are some visitors to see you,' she added.

Joshua stared at her, open-mouthed. Visitors? For him?

The whispering in the class turned to a buzz. 'Silence, class.' Sister Mary clapped her hands. 'Now, who can tell me which country has Harare as its capital?'

'Zimbabwe,' muttered Sister Martha, leading him out of the classroom, one hand at the back of his head. He had to hurry to keep up with her as she marched down the long verandah. The wooden rosary hanging from her girdle swung and clattered with each step. She seemed upset about something.

They reached the door of Reverend Mother's office. Sister Martha stopped and pulled his shirt straight. 'I don't like it,' she said under her breath. She smoothed his shorts. 'They're good, decent people but if they think they can just march in here – just two letters and a week's visit –' she broke off when she saw Joshua's questioning look. 'It's not right.' She smoothed his hair. 'I don't know why I'm bothering to tidy you up. Right,' she said crossly. She turned him to face the door, and knocked.

'Enter.'

Sister Martha ushered him in. Inside, behind a desk, sat Reverend Mother, her face all wrinkles. Joshua had only ever seen her in chapel; she did no teaching.

'Good morning, Reverend Mother,' he said politely, eyes to the ground.

She got up and came over to him. He was surprised to see how short she was next to him, and her usually stern face was smiling. 'Here,' she said, turning him towards the corner.

He hadn't noticed the man and woman sitting in chairs. Now they stood up and came forward.

'This is Mr and Mrs Nettar.'

It was the tourist couple.

'Say good morning to them,' she prompted.

'Good morning.'

'Hello, Yoswa,' they answered, in his language.

Joshua almost laughed; the way they spoke sounded so funny.

'I understand you have already met these people,' Reverend Mother said. 'Is that right, Joshua?'

He nodded. 'And I've been for a ride in their car,' he informed her proudly.

She smiled faintly. 'Have you, indeed.' She and Sister Martha exchanged glances. 'Well,' she went on, 'they have come here because they want to adopt a child, someone to go and live with them. They have a big house, with plenty of room. They want to adopt you, Joshua.'

Adoption? He looked at her in astonishment, and

then at the couple. The woman's lips twitched upwards in a nervous smile. The man nodded at him.

'Now, this is an important decision,' Reverend Mother went on, her hand still on his shoulder. 'Joshua – are you listening?'

But he was already imagining that boat-bed in the room high up in the big house. 'Yes, Mother John,' he said obediently.

'They have no children of their own and they've asked specially for you. You'd go to school in their country and grow up with them. And you'd learn their language, of course. They say you've already seen photographs of their house. Is that right?'

He nodded, hopping from one leg to the other, only hearing half of what she was saying as she continued to talk. The room would be all his. He tried to picture that: books and a clock.

'You don't have to say yes straight away,' she went on.

'No, don't rush,' Sister Martha chimed in. 'Just because they're in a hurry doesn't mean we have to be.'

'Sister –' Reverend Mother raised a hand to stop her. 'It is for the *boy* to decide, is it not? Now,' she turned to Joshua again, 'If you want to go with them, we are happy for you. Take your time.'

'It means you'll have to leave here.' Sister Martha spoke again.

Joshua nodded. Exactly. Where the tourists lived,

people probably wouldn't know about mountain men, he thought. If he went with them, he could carve without feeling he was doing something wrong. That would show Robert, and the others. He tried to imagine what it would be like sleeping alone and his head whirled with the excitement of it all.

He went over to the man and woman and looked back at the nuns. Sister Martha reached out a hand, then let it drop. There was an expression on her face that he couldn't read.

'Does this mean that you have made your choice?' Reverend Mother asked. 'Does this mean that you want to go with them?'

Joshua grinned. 'Yes,' he said excitedly.

The man spoke some foreign words. Mother John answered him hesitantly in the same language. She turned to Joshua. 'I've told him that you've said yes,' she said. 'Are you quite, quite sure?'

'Yes,' Joshua answered again. The man and woman hadn't even asked him what kind of man his father had been. It wouldn't matter. 'Oh yes.'

Sister Martha turned away.

'Josh! Josh! Where are you going?' Marius and Vincent came running after him. 'Can we come too?'

'If you want. I'm going to find Millie.' He had wanted to tell Robert about the adoption, but every time he'd tried, Robert had moved away to talk to someone else. So Millie would have to do. At least she knew the foreigners.

Millie was at the jetty, as he'd hoped she would be, with Tom and their father. He had bought an outboard motor, secondhand, and was cleaning and oiling it. When she saw Joshua coming, Millie left them to it.

'You mean you'll be going to live with them? In that big house?' Millie breathed, eyes wide, when he'd told her.

'Yes.'

'Can I come and stay?'

'Of course,' he promised, drawing himself up to his full height.

'What big house?' Marius asked.

Millie explained to him about the photographs. 'Why did they want you?' she asked Joshua. 'Why not me? They know me too.'

'I expect it's because you're not an orphan,' Marius said importantly, reminding her. 'Joshua is and I am, and Catherine. So's Vincent.'

Vincent nodded. 'Orphan,' he said gravely, pointing at himself.

'Orphans sometimes get adopted, Sister Martha says.' Marius frowned, uncertain about whether he would like that. 'She says not usually from so far away.' His face cleared as an explanation struck him. 'Maybe they wanted Joshua because he's not really one of us. He carves.'

There was a tiny silence. Millie looked curiously at Joshua. 'Do you?' she asked. 'Like mountain men?'

He shook his head. 'No,' he said.

'Ooh!' Marius squealed. 'Liar!'

Joshua glared at him.

'You're a mountain man! You're a liar! Mountain man! Liar!' Marius took Vincent's hand and the two of them jigged about, grinning.

'Stop it!' Millie scolded. 'Does Robert know?' she asked Joshua.

Know what? Joshua wondered. About the carving, or about the adoption? He shook his head a second time.

Millie's father came up to them, Tom by his side. 'What was that racket all about?' he asked Vincent, who was still jigging up and down, chanting silently.

Vincent opened his mouth to answer but was quelled by Millie's glare.

Millie's father looked round at them, amused. 'I see you've got yourself some brothers at last, Josh. Well done. That'll be fun for you. Now then, I've got room for three if any of you want to join me in the boat.'

Marius and Vincent set off at a run towards the boat. 'Right, that's two. And you, Josh? Hopeless as you are.

Tom, you've got other things to do. Millie? I expect I can squeeze you in.' He cuffed her affectionately.

They bundled in and, for once, Joshua cast off from the jetty without losing his balance. Marius and Vincent were silenced, in awe at the unexpected treat: a boat, and a boat with an outboard motor at that. Joshua looked at them with new eyes. Brothers, Millie's father had said. He hadn't thought of them that way. He had always wanted brothers.

CHAPTER EIGHTEEN

Down in the playground, six figures gathered around a nun, each with a small bag in their hand. As she dismissed them they darted away like a shoal of fish, their faded T-shirts and dresses almost merging with the dusty brown of the playground. A seventh figure, Joshua, stood apart from them up in the shade of the verandah, away from their chatter, dressed in white. A nun was bending over his foot.

One strap tightened. 'This is how you fasten them,' Sister Martha explained, but he couldn't really see his feet because her white, veiled head was hiding the stiff new sandals from him. When she had finished one sandal he stamped his foot. The leather made a sharp thud on the floor.

Behind her, the others were being rounded up by Sister Mary and Sister Maria Lisa, so that they could leave for the special Easter picnic. Joshua wriggled.

'Stand still,' Sister Martha ordered, tugging the other strap through the buckle. 'You're a lucky boy,' she said firmly.

'Bye, Josh!' Marius called.

Joshua waved.

'Bye, bye!' called Vincent. 'Bye, Josh!' called the others in turn.

He'd been looking forward to the picnic. He half wished the couple were coming for him the next day. But he called cheerfully back at the other orphans and waved as they left.

'I must just make sure Sister Maria Lisa's got the corned beef. Don't move,' Sister Martha said, and jumped down from the verandah after them.

He wriggled his toes. The leather of the new sandals rubbed against them. He bent and fumbled with the buckle, undid it and slipped one off.

'What are you doing?' Sister Martha said, returning.

'I'm taking off the sandals,' he answered. 'I don't like them.'

'Well, you're going to have to get used to them,' she said sharply. 'Put it on again. You'll be wearing shoes every day now – sandals in summer and shoes with laces in the winter, and socks. And sweaters. It's cold where you're going. And there are proper streets and houses made with bricks. And libraries,' she added wistfully. She tugged the buckle tight again. 'You won't be able to wander about without shoes as you do here.'

He found that difficult to imagine. When he had pictured where he was going to be living he hadn't got any further than the bedroom. 'I'll be able to swim, won't I?'

She looked doubtful. 'I don't know, chick. Maybe there'll be a swimming pool nearby.'

'What's wrong with the sea?'

'Too cold in winter,' she said abruptly. 'And it's probably dirty. Anyway, I don't know that they live anywhere near the sea.'

He didn't like the sound of that.

She stood back and looked at him critically. 'There, you'll do,' she said, tweaking his collar. 'Now, no going outside and messing up your clothes, hmm? Wait here for them.'

He nodded.

'I don't know what's keeping them,' she said crossly. But still she hovered. 'I have to go.'

He knew she did. After all, she was the one who organised the picnic.

'I'm sure they'll be here soon.' She sounded almost as nervous as he felt. 'Reverend Mother says you'll have a better life with them,' she said.

He nodded again. He didn't know what that meant. But at least he wouldn't be the odd one out, he thought.

She swooped down and hugged him, almost suffocating him in the starchy folds of her habit. 'Goodbye,' she said, smoothing the hair from his eyes. 'You're a lucky boy, Josh' she repeated, more fiercely this time, as if she was trying to convince herself. 'Just think, they want you so much they've come halfway round the world for you. Always remember that. They've even paid for you.' She paused, and then went on, almost to herself, 'It's easy if you think everything in life can be bought. Far too easy and far too quick.'

Joshua blinked at her. 'I'll come back, won't I?' he interrupted. 'They'll bring me back? I won't be gone for ever?'

She didn't answer. 'Be good,' she said, her eyes moist.

He flung his arms around her, not wanting her to go, but she did all the same, in a flurry of white and a clatter of rosary beads.

He was alone.

He decided to carry his bundle along the verandah to the main entrance. It wasn't heavy; all it had gained was another comic from Millie and a prayer book from the nuns. He went back for Pig and set him facing the doorway, standing squarely on his wooden trotters, with the bundle propped on his back. He thought again about the beautiful bedroom he'd have all to himself. His stomach churned, partly in excitement, partly in fear.

They were coming for him in the car, Sister Martha had said. He left the doorway and wandered down to where the white jasmine marked the edge of the school, and looked down the road, first to the left, then to the right, but there was no car to be seen.

He jumped experimentally in his new sandals. Dust

flew up and settled on the leather. He struggled with the buckles and took them off and jumped again. There, that was better. He left the sandals lying on the ground and went back to Pig, untied his bundle and took out the comic.

I'll look at the comic, he thought, then I'll check the road again. If they haven't come by then, I'll still be able to catch up with the others.

He sat down, leaning against Pig, and flicked open the comic.

He put it down. No, I won't, he thought, they don't want me on the picnic, not really. Besides, he'd said goodbye.

He went back for his sandals and was putting them on again when he heard the sound of a car approaching. Hurriedly he tried to buckle the sandals, but gave up when he couldn't get his fingers to move quickly enough. He shuffled to the doorway to pick up his things and set off back across the short stretch of ground towards the gleaming car, bundle in one hand. With the other arm he half-carried, half-dragged Pig, his body twisting with the effort.

The man took his bundle. The woman named Marguerite removed her sunglasses and hugged him and he smiled up at her, excited again, his misgivings forgotten. He was going to a better life. Sister Martha had said so.

'Get in, dear,' the woman said.

He climbed on to the back seat. She closed his door, and the man turned on the engine. He sniffed the lovely smell of leather again and gazed once more at the dials.

Something was missing.

Pig! Pig was still outside in the road. He pressed down on the door handle to open it.

The woman turned and closed it again and locked it. 'Careful,' she said.

'But – Pig.'

He thought she understood, but the car was drawing away. She shook her head gently at him. 'We can't take that,' she said. 'Wherever would we put it? Anyway, how would we get it on the aeroplane?'

Joshua just heard words. They meant nothing. He turned round and knelt on the back seat as he had done with Millie. He couldn't see Pig. He'd been swallowed up in swirls of sand as the car sprang forward. He turned back and tapped the woman on the shoulder. 'I want Pig,' he said, loudly and clearly.

She just smiled at him.

He slumped back on the seat. Wind from the open car window lifted the hair from his neck and blew the woman's hair around her face. She put a hand up and held it still. Then she turned and indicated that he should wind up the window. 'It's too draughty,' she said.

He stared at her. 'Pig,' he mouthed, willing her to react.

'Close it,' she said, miming the action. When he did nothing, she sighed, and wound up the window herself.

They drove past the rubbish heap. Without the air from the windows, it was stifling inside the car. The man and woman were talking quietly. Joshua didn't understand a word. A better life. He hadn't thought beyond that. It had all happened too quickly. Now Sister Martha's other words rang in his ears: shoes the whole time, socks, no sea. He hadn't realised. It was uncomfortable in his sandals. He kicked them off. 'The other side of the world,' Sister Martha had said. No Pig, he thought.

By now they were approaching the hospital building.

He reached out his left hand and, very carefully, lifted the knob on the door that he'd seen the woman press down. His heart thudded and the blood roared in his ears.

Ahead of them Swabber put one paw in the road and began limping across, not looking to left or right.

The man braked and the car slowed almost to a stop. Joshua pressed down on the door handle and pushed. It flew open. He landed awkwardly on one knee, then jumped to his feet, not looking round, and ran.

He heard shouts behind him, a car door slamming and the sound of heavy footsteps.

Joshua ran even faster, tring to work out his escape route in his head as he ran. If he continued on by the hospital he'd come to the row of small shops and the market and they'd find him again. And he couldn't go back. He dithered, then swerved to the left and struck off, crashing through the oleander bushes.

Sweet, musty scent broke over him in a wave. Twigs scratched his cheeks and his scalp. Pink blossom brushed his shoulders and fell to the ground as he passed. Instinctively, he went the way he'd seen his father go. Ahead of him was a belt of thicker bushes, their leaves dark green and glossy. He barged through those too, layer after layer of them, till they thinned out and he thought he saw a path, of sorts.

He had a stitch in his side. He stopped, panting, holding his ribs, and looked around him. A parrot screeched at him from a nearby tree, its eyes glittering wickedly from among gaudy green feathers. But that was the only sound. No twigs snapped behind him; there was no one following.

If he turned back, the couple would be waiting. He didn't dare try to sneak round to the beach where the others would be picknicking in case Sister brought him back. And if he went to Robert's house or to Millie's they might tell on him.

Above him the mountains loomed. His father had come from up there, even though he had never admitted it. He was on the path Robert said the mountain men took. That first mountain man with the berries would have come this way. If he went on far enough, he'd find them.

CHAPTER NINETEEN

The earth was dry and hard behind the belt of bushes. The rough path climbed gradually upwards, and so did Joshua. He was hungry. He hadn't eaten since breakfast and the sun was now high in the sky.

He caught his hand on a thorn bush. He stopped and sucked the scratch. When he looked up, he noticed a shelter, just a canopy stretched over poles, and, outside, a monkey playing. It had a banana in its hand.

He edged forward till he could see into the shelter. It was empty. The monkey was chained to one of the poles and hadn't seen him. It let the banana fall and dug its fingers into its fur, looking for fleas.

Joshua leaped for the banana and retreated with it. He sat down to eat at a safe distance from the monkey.

The monkey was furious. It jabbered at him and waved its fist.

Joshua peeled the banana and gulped it down.

The monkey hurled itself forward as far as its chain would permit.

Joshua flinched. Then he grinned. It couldn't reach him.

The monkey danced back angrily on its chain and lurched forward again.

But Joshua was not going to be frightened away.

At last it gave up. It stared with sad worried eyes at Joshua then sat down on its thin, wrinkled bottom and began picking fleas from its mangy skin.

Joshua got up, set his face towards the mountain and began to trudge upwards once more. After another hour he was still passing scattered thorn bushes and stunted trees and the mountains seemed just as high above him as they had when he started. He wasn't used to climbing. His legs ached, his mouth was dry, his head pounded.

A shadow fell on the path. At the end of the shadow walked a man in a blanket and conical hat.

Joshua waited nervously. The man's strides slowed as he approached.

Joshua bowed. 'Hello,' he said, 'My name's Joshua.'

The man stopped.

'My father was a mountain man.' There, it was out. A weight lifted from him. He went on. 'He's dead now. Can I come to your village?'

The man was puzzled. He took his water bottle from his belt and handed it over with a curt bow. Perhaps it was water that the boy from the coast wanted.

Joshua seized the bottle and drank greedily. He wiped his mouth with the back of his hand. 'They wanted to adopt me,' he told the man, returning the bottle. 'But I ran away. Can I come and live with you?'

The man opened his mouth and spoke.

Joshua's face clouded over. He didn't understand any of the words; they just sounded like grunts.

The man stopped talking and waved an arm at Joshua, then pointed to the ground and back down at the coast.

Joshua thought he was telling him to wait. 'All right,' he said.

The mountain man turned on his heel and went back up the trail as swiftly and silently as he had come. He was going to tell the others, Joshua thought, and then he'd be back for him. He sat down to wait. He waited so patiently and quietly that a lizard came close to his feet, paused, then scurried lightly up his leg and on to his elbow where it was resting on his knee. They stared at each other before Joshua shook it off.

He looked back up the path. It was empty and the shadows were lengthening as the evening came on. On impulse, he gathered small stones together and made a circle with an arrow inside, pointing downwards. Then he set off at a run, back to the monkey. It would be less lonely to wait with the monkey to keep him company.

The animal was not pleased to see him again. It chattered angrily and bared its teeth. Careful to keep it at a distance, Joshua circled the shelter, looking for more food or water. In the corner, on a stone, he saw a bag. He darted at it, and was out of the monkey's reach before it could react. The monkey screamed in fury.

Joshua unwrapped the sacking. Inside there was no food, just a knife, its blade shiny and well cared for. He rested the blade in his hand.

'Calm down,' he said to the monkey, which was dancing up and down, still screaming.

Joshua ignored it. He scrabbled around, looking for wood and found a piece about a foot long that felt good when he picked it up. He sat on a flat stone near the end of the monkey's chain and began to cut and whittle.

The sound seemed to soothe the creature. It still looked worriedly at Joshua, but it sat down now and picked at itself as before, looking at him every time it raised a flea to its mouth, keeping him under surveillance.

A pointed head emerged from the wood, then one crooked foot and another. Joshua held the lizard in his imagination as he carved. He worked on down the body, making it twist slightly as if it was running.

Above him the sky was darkening. The heavens opened and rain poured down on the mountain in great vertical sheets of water. Trapped on its chain, the monkey was sodden in a matter of seconds, the rain running down his fur in torrents. Although Joshua was standing only a few feet away, the spot where he stood was still dry. It was like watching the monkey through a glass wall. He reached out and put his arm into the wall. The rain wet it up to the elbow. He pulled it back and watched the drops of water evaporate on his skin.

Abruptly the rain stopped. Steam rose from the ground in front of him. The monkey, which had curled up in a ball when the rain came, raised its head and shook water from its fur. Joshua put the knife to the wood again. He shaped out a third leg and a fourth. And still no one came to bring him to the mountains.

He looked up towards the peaks, which showed black against the deep purple of the setting sun. The temperature was dropping. Joshua wished he had his bundle of belongings with him so he could have put on a second shirt. He carved out a tiny powerful tail and shivered. Why was no one coming? He got up. Perhaps he'd better go back to where he'd met the mountain man. He tucked his shirt inside his shorts and put the wooden lizard down his front. Then he wrapped up the knife, laid it on the stone, and set his face back towards the mountains.

He felt small and exposed in the clear moonlight. Each thorn bush looked the same as the last, and it was difficult to see the path. He stopped, pursed his lips and whistled, once, twice, sending the sound sharply into the still air, the way his father had taught him.

There was no answering whistle.

He no longer knew if he was on the right trail. There weren't even any bushes with berries as he'd expected. Which must mean, he realised, that he still had a long way to go.

A solitary tree blocked his path. He didn't remember going past a tree before. He rested his forehead on the rough bark and his bottom lip trembled. He was so tired. He slid down the trunk and curled up at its base, making himself as small as possible. Faintly, far below, he thought he could hear the sound of waves breaking.

CHAPTER TWENTY

Twigs snapped and leaves rustled as a man in a conical hat picked his way through the undergrowth. In his arms he carried a large bundle – a bundle totally covered up by the blanket that hung from his shoulders, except for two bare, brown legs that dangled down. It was difficult to see here in the darkness where the leaves shut out the moonlight. He carried on, trusting to memory and smell, and reached the oleanders.

He paused. There was a path to the right and he took it. A dog appeared out of the darkness, raised its muzzle and sniffed, nostrils quivering. It whined quietly. It limped towards the man, whined again and began to walk ahead of him. It turned, making sure that he was following, and led him on to a cluster of small houses around a wide, dusty clearing. No lamps or candles burned in the darkness; everyone was sleeping. Except for one. As Swabber walked across to the stone shop, she came from the doorway where she'd been watching and shuffled towards the man.

He took a step back, holding tightly to the bundle in his arms. She signed to him that she meant him no harm. This time he let her approach. She lifted the corner of his blanket and looked beneath. Then she smiled – a toothless, shy smile – and touched the mountain man by the hand. Beckoning him to follow, she led him a short distance back the way he had come. Swabber limped alongside.

They reached jasmine bushes. 'Put him down,' she said, gesturing.

Something hard and wooden dug into Joshua's stomach. Scratchy wool rubbed his cheeks and arm. He recognised a sweet fragrance as he was set on his feet. He opened his eyes and saw the mountain man bending over him. He could hear the sea. The man touched Joshua's head lightly, bowed, and left.

A hand held his. Old Mama Siska led him towards the convent where lights still shone. He stumbled with tiredness and only dimly saw a rush of white as Sister Martha caught him and picked him up.

He heard murmuring above his head. 'Ouf, he's quite a weight.'

'What else do you expect?' said another.

'Drink,' Sister Mary's voice said, and sweet, warm liquid was put to his lips. The voices receded again and he was carried to bed and undressed. Something fell out of his shirt on to the bed. There was a small gasp. Then he felt it being put in his hand, and his fingers closed over the rough lizard. He grasped it tightly as he was helped into bed. His head touched something hard and smooth. His eyes flickered open and glimpsed Pig.

'Marius and Vincent put him there,' he heard Sister Martha's whisper. 'Hoping he'd come back.'

He fell asleep again at once, Pig standing guard.

CHAPTER TWENTY-ONE

'Up, all of you! Up!'

Joshua heard the call and the clap of Sister Martha's hands.

'Come along, Joshua!'

He threw back the sheet and got out of bed and joined the others.

'God bless to us this day,' Sister Martha said.

'And ourselves to His service. Amen,' they chorused back.

'Breakfast in ten minutes.'

It was a day like every day in the orphanage. He splashed water on his face and his neck and arms. They were scratched from the thorns. When he saw Marius looking at the scratches he grinned. Younger brother, he thought, pleased. He cupped water in his hands and threw it at him.

Marius ran, squealing.

He sat down at his place at the table and, as usual, forgot to pass the teapot until one of the girls reminded him, and, of course, was one of the last to finish what was in his bowl.

There was a rustle from behind and Sister Martha leaned between him and Marius. 'Joshua, when you've finished, I want you to come with me to Reverend Mother's study.'

Joshua put down his spoon. 'Why?' he asked.

'Mr and Mrs Nettar are here.'

The others round the long table had stopped talking and were listening, agog.

Joshua began to shake. 'I want to stay here,' he said.

'I know you do.' Her mouth was set in a grim line. 'Aren't you going to finish that?' She pointed at the food left in his bowl.

He shook his head. His appetite had vanished.

'Then we may as well go now.'

He followed her out to the passage.

'Hello, Josh.'

He was startled to see Robert. 'Hello.'

Robert brought his hands out from behind his back. 'Here,' he said, handing over a small newspaper bundle. 'I was keeping them safe for you.'

Joshua unwrapped the paper. Inside, to his amazement, were his knife and the piece of wood. When he looked up, Robert was smiling at him. He bundled them up again and smiled back. 'Thanks.'

'I didn't know if you'd come back,' his friend went on. 'Sister Martha came and told us last night you'd gone. Mum says she's making your biscuits and will you come and have some this afternoon after school?'

Joshua nodded. His eyes slid up to Sister Martha's. 'Can I?' he asked.

'Would you like Robert to come with you to Reverend Mother?'

His mouth went dry again. He nodded. She hadn't answered his question. He held the bundle tightly as they walked.

Robert nudged him. 'She cried when she came to our house last night,' he whispered.

Joshua digested this piece of information. He hadn't ever seen anyone cry over him.

Three faces turned towards them when they entered Reverend Mother's study. The man and woman looked tired and tense. They were holding hands tightly. Joshua concentrated on looking at Mother John, as if by doing that, he could shut out the strangers.

She examined him, her eyes hard and piercing. Finally she spoke. 'We have been discussing you,' she said. 'Mr and Mrs Nettar are upset that you ran away. Very upset indeed.'

Joshua waited. At his side, Robert was still too.

'We've also been talking to Sister Martha. She thinks it may not be such a good idea for you to leave us.'

His heart did a tiny skip.

'But,' she went on, 'they have adopted you, and you did say yes.'

Joshua drooped. Behind him, Sister Martha rested a hand lightly on his shoulder.

'You must learn not to say yes without thinking.'

He moved backwards, closer to Sister Martha, and Robert shuffled nearer.

'They have come a long way to fetch you.'

'That's not Joshua's fault!' Robert burst out.

'Thank you, Robert,' she said drily. 'Just what I was about to say. You are a very fortunate boy, Joshua.'

Oh no, he thought, remembering Sister Martha's words the morning before. He didn't want to go with the strangers. He knew that now; he didn't want that bed, he didn't want to go.

'Mr and Mrs Nettar have missed one flight already. They have to leave this afternoon, and they would still like to take you.'

He froze.

'If you would like to go. But Sister Martha has advised them that this would be a mistake.' He held his breath. 'And I have told them that I agree with her.'

He stared at Mother John, not daring to believe.

'Now, Joshua. I'm going to ask you again. Would you like these good people to adopt you?'

He looked straight into her eyes and shook his head.

'What did you say?' she asked sharply.

'No, Reverend Mother,' he answered, trying desperately to hide the quiver in his voice.

'Have you anything else to say?'

He didn't dare.

Sister Martha opened her mouth.

'No, Sister,' Reverend Mother said sharply. 'Let the boy speak for himself. Now, Joshua,' her voice softened. 'Would you like to stay with us?'

'Yes, please, Reverend Mother,' he said eagerly

'And there'll be no more running away? No more escaping?'

He shook his head.

Joshua watched her turn to the foreign couple and speak to them in their language. The man protested but the woman said something that made him lower his head to hers and rest it there.

Reverend Mother turned to face Joshua once more and regarded him gravely. Then her stern, wrinkled face eased. 'You may stay.'

'Oh!' Joshua's face split right across in a huge and happy smile. He turned and buried himself in Sister Martha's arms.

'Joshua.'

Sister Martha turned him back to face Reverend Mother.

'Don't you think you should say something to Mr and Mrs Nettar?' the older nun prompted.

He left the safety of Sister Martha and Robert and went and stood nervously in front of the couple.

The woman's eyes were wet. She reached out, and he let her pull him to her and hug him. The bundle with the knife dug into her side and she looked down in surprise.

His nervousness left him. He drew back and, slowly, he unwrapped the paper once more. He took the piece of wood and held it out to her. 'I can carve,' he said to her and the man. 'See?' He pointed to the emerging head. He pressed it into her hand. 'You can have it, if you like.'

The room was very silent. 'You can take it with you,' he said, in case she hadn't understood. He looked round.

Robert was the first to speak. 'Mountain man,' he teased, but gently, and there was a grin on his face.

Joshua grinned back.

'*Our* mountain man,' Sister Martha corrected.

Joshua's chin lifted. 'No,' he said. 'I'm just Joshua.'

A Note from the Author

Dear Reader,

After his father's death, Joshua thinks that he doesn't belong anywhere. It's a feeling many of us have, perhaps if we're foreign, perhaps just if we're different. It's certainly something I experienced when I was Joshua's age – which is maybe one of the reasons for writing this book.

When I was eleven I was sent away from the tropics where I lived, to go to boarding school in Wales. School was fine, but for the first two years I didn't see my parents. I stayed with relations in the holidays, but it was confusing; they didn't do things the way we did at home, and I didn't know where I belonged – a bit like Joshua when he discovers his background.

After being in a hot, tropical country where all the colours were bright and the smells were strong and the sea just there for the swimming, coming to Europe was like being dumped in an icy bath in a grey room. It took me some time to get used to it, but later I grew to love it. And if it was hard for me, who had experience of living in Britain before, imagine how difficult it might have been for Joshua who had never travelled anywhere, who wouldn't have known what to expect.

As Joshua found out, people can be peculiar about other people who aren't the same. Joshua thought being adopted would solve his problems. In the end, though, he decided to stay where he was, to acknowledge what he was, even if it was a bit different.

It's good to be a little different from each other. Wouldn't the world be dull if we were all the same?

Best wishes,